A WHISPERED QUESTION

With unspoken consent, they lingered behind the others, watching the musicians put their violins away and retreat down the back staircase. For a moment they made idle conversation.

Lady Landor, he agreed, was showing herself to extraordinary good effect. "Everyone I have heard speaking of her has said that she is charming," Lord Cardross said in a low voice. "No one here tonight is ill bred enough to speak openly of any scandal. You may not want advice of me, Miss Rogers," he told her. "But I will give it all the same. You must prepare yourself, quite privately, for the eventuality that some of what scandal has been spread about Lady Landor may be true."

Other Avon Books by
Valerie Bradstreet

THE FORTUNE WHEEL

THE IVORY FAN

VALERIE BRADSTREET

AVON
PUBLISHERS OF BARD, CAMELOT, DISCUS AND FLARE BOOKS

THE IVORY FAN is an original publication of Avon Books.
This work has never before appeared in book form.

AVON BOOKS
A division of
The Hearst Corporation
959 Eighth Avenue
New York, New York 10019

First Avon Printing, January, 1982

AVON TRADEMARK REG. U. S. PAT. OFF. AND IN
OTHER COUNTRIES, MARCA REGISTRADA, HECHO EN U. S. A.

Printed in the U. S. A.

WFH 10 9 8 7 6 5 4 3 2 1

Chapter One

"WHAT on earth can have possessed your father, my dear Louisa?" Mrs. Thrasher demanded, making a great commotion with her fan in her dismay. "How he ever could have left you in the company of that woman, I will never understand. Her own reputation is already ruined and now she will ruin yours, as well!"

It was so much what Louisa had been afraid the older woman had wanted to tell her when she had proposed their promenade that she had difficulty in suppressing a sigh. Mrs. Thrasher had taken her arm as they walked down the gravel path toward the span of water which rested, like a blue diamond, in the green velvet palm of the hand of St. James's Park. Behind them, up and down the dusty Mall, a great procession of all types and varieties of carriages creaked and groaned as they traveled about in order to make the best display of their passengers, all members of London's *haut ton*.

"But Lady Landor is quite charming," the girl protested. "When you meet her, Mrs. Thrasher, you will see that . . ."

"I scarcely think I will take advantage of *that* opportunity, my dear," her companion replied. "Indeed, if I had not promised your headmistress that I would keep an eye on you during your stay in the city, it might well have been that our paths never would have crossed. I do not think it likely that Lady Landor and I move in quite the same company. At least that is what I propose to believe until she has established herself socially. It is all very well to belong to the elite in Florence. London is quite another matter. And besides, her husband, the Duke, is dead."

And, looking down her nose in just such a way as to make it certain that the girl would take her meaning, she paused to admire a bush of roses with the air of one passing an aesthetic judgment on nature. It had taken an great deal of gray silk to outfit her stout person, and she wheezed and puffed so from the slight amount of ex-

5

ercise they had taken that the cloth threatened, at times, to split at the seams.

"However that may be, Mrs. Thrasher," Louisa replied more stiffly, "the fact is that my father, Captain Rogers, means to marry Lady Landor and when he wrote to me at Miss Patterson's academy, he made it clear that it was his wish that she see to my coming out during his absence from the country."

Clearly Mrs. Thrasher was not accustomed to even the mildest sort of disagreement. A self-satisfied expression had engraved itself on her broad face and even the feathers in her turban seemed to declare a certain moral superiority.

"Lady Landor is reputed to be the worst sort of flirt, my dear," she declared. "There! You must know the worst, although it pains me to have to tell you. Mark my words! Nothing will come of their engagement. When your papa returns from the Peninsula campaign—God willing—he will realize that he has placed you in the worst possible hands."

"Perhaps when Miss Patterson wrote to you, Mrs. Thrasher," Louisa said with cool deliberation, "and so kindly asked you to keep an eye on me in London, she did not mention my extreme fondness for my father and my absolute confidence in his good judgment."

She was a dark-haired beauty with a natural flush of color in her cheeks and blue eyes which were so thickly fringed as to make them appear to be extraordinarily intense. Nothing could have been more demure than the white sprigged muslin dress that she was wearing, caught high above the waist with a blue ribbon which matched the one wound around the crown of her poke bonnet, but it was clear from the very way she held herself, as well as from what she said, that she had a will of her own.

The company inside the park that afternoon was quite as fashionable as that riding on The Mall on its west side. The older woman and the girl were passed by a gentleman who dressed according to the Brummel fashion with his coattails cut square and the sleeves padded at the top to produce the popular kick-up effect. The lady with him had completed her outfit with pink suede gloves which ended at her elbows and a capote hat to match. The sight of them put Louisa in mind of the costume Lady Landor had been donning when Louisa had left the house to join Mrs. Thrasher earlier in the afternoon. Lady Landor was very partial to her daily ride up and down The Mall in her fashionable equipage, and

Louisa did not like to think what Mrs. Thrasher would say if she caught sight of her guardian today.

"Miss Patterson wrote me that you were headstrong," Mrs. Thrasher replied with a frown which furrowed her broad forehead like a hayfield in spring. "Intelligent and headstrong. Those were her very words. You must watch yourself, my dear. In this society, both of those characteristics rank as distinct disadvantages as far as young ladies are concerned. But, no matter. What can I say to persuade you to leave that woman's house immediately and come to me?"

Out of respect for the absent Miss Patterson who had been her mentor and friend for years, Louisa did not turn on one wedge-shaped heel and leave Mrs. Thrasher behind as she would dearly have liked to do. If she had only guessed, when she had received that lady's note this morning, introducing herself and suggesting this promenade, that she would be urged to go against her father's wishes, she never would have agreed to walk in St. James's Park. Doubtless her headmistress had had the best of motives when she had written to Mrs. Thrasher, but Louisa was certain that Miss Patterson never could have guessed that the woman would make such a hue and cry about the position in which Louisa found herself.

Three weeks ago, when the letter had come from her father, Louisa had not been unduly surprised to discover that, after so many years, he had found someone he wished to marry. She had been seven when her mother, a pale and patient woman long since resigned to wait in the country for her husband to return from yet another secret military mission, had fallen victim to a fever and had subsequently died. Captain Rogers had grieved for her, but he was a handsome man who liked good company, and Louisa, from the safety of the young lady's academy to which she had been consigned, had long since expected him to make a new alliance.

Her father had written to her at the academy to say that he and Lady Landor had met under the most romantic conditions.

"She was widowed a year ago in Florence," he had written in his familiar scrawl, "and was finally—after an illness brought on by her loss—making her return to England after fifteen years spent abroad. Because of Napoleon, of course, it seemed wisest to make that return by sea. As for me, Wellington had sent me back to England on a mission. The Bay of Biscay was stormy, as it usually is. Besides the sailors, she and I were the only ones above deck.

7

She is an extraordinary woman, my dear, and I want you to be fond of her. She will not try to become your mother. Indeed, I must confess, she is only fifteen years your elder. But she is wise in the world's ways from necessity. You will please me by accepting her guidance in everything until my return."

Louisa had felt no resentment. More than anything she wanted her father to be happy. If he had married someone younger—well, that was only to be expected. Many other gentlemen did the same. And she was encouraged by the fact that Lady Landor had no wish to play the role of mother. At eighteen, Louisa would far rather have a friend. And yet, despite these self-assurances, despite the fact that, in a postscript, her father had warned her not to expect someone quite "ordinary," Louisa had been taken completely by surprise.

Perhaps the lavish appointments of the lady's house in Grosvenor Square should have hinted at her exotic personality, for the drawing room in which Louisa waited had been decorated in the Oriental fashion which was rising on a wave of popularity, and there were gilt dragons everywhere and magnificent great jars, not to mention the delicately lacquered furniture and the richly colored carpets. And yet, when Lady Landor had swept into that curiously exotic room, Louisa had been astonished. Granted that twelve years had passed since her father had been widowed. Granted that, whenever he was in England, he lived among the *haut ton*. Still, she had not expected anyone as vivid as Lady Landor, with her masses of chestnut hair and her brown eyes and milk-white skin.

It was not only Lady Landor's appearance which amazed the girl, it was her general manner. Indeed, she greeted Louisa as though they were already friends. "And we might as well be," she had declared, "for I have heard so much about you from your father that I feel I know you very well. Poor you are at a disadvantage with only a letter to introduce me. Your father wanted to be here when we met, you know, but off he had to go to Spain. I never trust the military to do anything that is expected of them. A bunch of great boys playing spies and soldiers, I told your father. I so like to amuse him."

Indeed, amusement was Lady Landor's forte, it seemed, for she confided in Louisa without delay that she was as frivolous as could be. "What fun it will be to introduce you to society," she had delcared that morning as they sat together over tea. "I have always wanted to plan a coming out, but until I met your father and found

8

out about you, it did not seem that there would ever be such an opportunity. Besides, my first marriage kept me in Florence, for my husband was so fond of that particular city that he never would agree to stay anywhere else. And the Italians arrange things quite differently.''

Confidences poured out of Lady Landor in a stream. Her marriage to a duke had been arranged. ''I never loved him in the romantic way,'' she told Louisa. ''But he was rich. And, of course, there was the title. He liked me to be ornamental, and it pleased him so much when I obliged him that it has become a habit with me.''

It had seemed to Louisa a touching story in its way, and she wondered if perhaps her father had not felt the same. Lady Landor, however, seemed to find nothing sad in the sacrifice of her youth and had gone on contentedly.

''Fortunately,'' she said, ''my former husband left me very well provided for, which is a mercy since I have become accustomed to as much luxury as possible and hate to count the cost. I feel that I have earned it, you know, although your father warned me that perhaps I ought not to put it just that way. Still, it is so difficult to consider what one is about to say. In Florence there was no difficulty because I never learned Italian and when I rattled on in English, speaking my mind, not one of my husband's friends could understand me. At least they pretended not to, which comes to much the same thing.''

There was, it seemed, no end to Lady Landor's frankness. She was marrying Louisa's father because she cared for him so deeply.

''One marriage of convenience is enough, my dear,'' she said. ''You must believe me when I tell you that I dote on your dear papa. Did he tell you, I wonder, how it was we happened to meet?''

Louisa had listened to the story of the sea-tossed meeting with her chin propped on her hands, wondering what it was about the older woman that made her seem so much larger than life. Perhaps it was her general expansiveness. Or perhaps it was the way she waved her hands like an actress. Even her voice was quite distinctive, for it struck a lower register than was common for ladies, and her words seemed to roll after one another like waves.

''I fell in love with him at once!'' she had declared, her large, brown eyes nearly liquid with emotion. ''And he with me.''

Everything was a hyperbole to Lady Landor, Louisa had discovered. No doubt her father found it amusing. In every way she could, the girl tried to see Lady Landor through his eyes. It was important to her to understand the precise nature of his attachment. The *true* attraction. Louisa knew her father well enough to be certain that beauty alone, or even charm, would make him capitulate after so many years.

Frankness. Generosity. And kindness. These were three attributes she could already ascribe to Lady Landor. When Mrs. Thrasher's invitation had arrived this morning, Lady Landor had made no protest that she had not been included.

"No doubt, if she is your headmistress's friend, she wants to talk about the school and . . . and all sorts of people I know nothing of," she had told Louisa with a smile. "Go with her and take a promenade. I will take the carriage out as usual, and be driven up and down The Mall. Such a delicious custom. I confess I do like to be seen. Any day now the invitations will start arriving, my dear, and we will be busy night and day."

Now, however, having talked to Mrs. Thrasher, Louisa was quite certain that would not be the case.

"Certainly the general run of society will refuse to receive her," the stout personage declared, turning back from the water where there was a view of Whitehall toward The Mall.

"But on what account?" Louisa demanded. "You have accused her of nothing worse than being a flirt, and although this is my first long stay in London, I cannot think that is uncommon."

"You are loyal to protect her," Mrs. Thrasher replied, nodding at a group of passersby. "You know, of course, she married for money. The Duke was much older than herself."

"She was only a young girl at the time, madam!" Louisa replied with warmth. "She followed her family's wishes. I know enough from reading novels to be certain *that* is not unusual."

"She subsequently led the Duke a merry chase," Mrs. Thrasher continued, inexorably puffing her way along the gravel path. "That is the word from Florence."

"Are you suggesting that she deceived her husband?" Louisa demanded, her temper thoroughly aroused.

"Good gracious, child!" was her reply. "That is a thing a gel like yourself should never ask. Never think of, for that matter! Lady Landor's influence is already apparent, I fear."

"I will not allow her to be slandered," Louisa retorted. "Someone has been busy tarnishing her name, and I intend to right the situation."

"But, of course, you can do nothing of the kind," Mrs. Thrasher told her condescendingly. "My experience with the world tells me that people bring the tales that are told about them on their own heads."

"And so you will believe everything you hear, without evidence?" Louisa said, not bothering to disguise the scorn in her voice. No doubt Mrs. Thrasher's report to Miss Patterson would not be reassuring, but she determined to send a letter of her own, explaining the true situation. It was unbearable that the woman her father intended to marry should have come to London to find her reputation lost already and that on the basis of idle rumor.

"The lady spells her own misfortune," Mrs. Thrasher said in a low voice, pointing with her fan. Turning, Louisa saw that Lady Landor was being driven along The Mall not a great distance from them. And they were not the first to notice. In all directions, heads were turned.

And, indeed, Lady Landor was worthy of attention. For the purpose of this public outing, she had chosen to hide her beautiful red hair under a green, silk turban, topped with two proud ostrich feathers, all of which was so much in the fashion that, in itself, it would not have attracted notice. But with her gown Lady Landor gave the extravagance of her nature its head, for the green silk was cut very high at the waist in the Empire fashion and lower at the neck than was quite usual for afternoon. The folds of the skirt were arranged in such a way as to reveal the fine lines of her figure as she reclined in her seat in a manner as to display her charms to best advantage.

"There! Do you see?" Lady Thrasher demanded. "How she flaunts her beauty! Like any common chit!"

"Envy is, no doubt, a common response, Mrs. Thrasher," Louisa said with a long, slow look at her companion which covered her from head to foot. "You will excuse me if I do not attend your further, but I will take advantage of more gracious company before I lose my manners completely. *That* is your influence, you see."

And, with that rejoinder, she stepped into The Mall and gestured in Lady Landor's direction. In an instant, a liveried footman was offering her a hand into the carriage.

"My dear!" Lady Landor cried. "How good to have you join me. But where is Mrs. Thrasher? Will you introduce me?"

"She is no one I would care to have you meet," Louisa replied with a toss of her black curls as she settled her white, muslin skirts about her. "It appears that she is not the sort of person either of us cares to know."

Chapter Two

INDEED, so angry had Mrs. Thrasher made Louisa that she could not face the prospect of remaining in the house later that afternoon, even though she should be resting for a ball that night at Almack's. As a consequence she threw on her cashmere shawl, tied a poke bonnet over her dark curls, and hurried over to the square where she could pace about all unconfined. But, before she could so much as turn a thought to the problem Mrs. Thrasher and others like her presented, she was accosted by a girl not so much older than herself, a thin-faced beauty dressed in an elegant manner in blue sprigged muslin and wearing the deepest bonnet Louisa had ever seen.

"Bonjour, mademoiselle," she said in a low, attractive voice with a mysterious ring about it, "you will forgive this intrusion, please? Allow me to introduce myself. My name is Michelle Rioux. My brother Claude and I have recently become your neighbors."

So taken by surprise was Louisa by this introduction that she would only incline her head. All of which did not deter the stranger from continuing with a certain note of urgency in her low voice.

"My brother is standing over there," she said, indicating a gentleman standing at the farther end of the square, so far distant that Louisa could not make out his features. "He will join us later if you will consent to talk to me about an important matter. First allow me to tell you that we are *agents provocateurs*."

On hearing this startling piece of information, Louisa raised one hand to her lips. She did not yet know much of London, but surely it was not the ordinary way of things that strangers should greet you in the park with the surprising news that they were spies.

"You will think I am mad," Mademoiselle Rioux said, with her charming accent becoming all the heavier. "But it is quite

13

true. We are French, my brother and I, as you will have assumed by now, I'm sure. Voila! We are French, but no supporters of Napoleon. That is not *de rigueur*, as so many Englishmen believe.''

Louisa found her voice at last. "But if this is true," she said, "why have you come to me? I am involved in nothing political. I applaud you and your brother if you avoid Napoleon, certainly. But I cannot understand . . ."

"Will you allow me to explain, mademoiselle?" her companion asked her, indicating a bench where they both could sit. "I will take little of your time, I assure you. But I am convinced that you will keep confidential anything that I may say."

"I think you are very reckless if you think that," Louisa told her, albeit taking the seat that had been indicated, her curiosity aroused. "Why, you know nothing of me except that I am, apparently, a neighbor."

"On the contrary, mademoiselle, *comme il faut*," Miss Rioux told her, sitting down beside her and smoothing the drapes of her elegant gown. "In other words, everything is as it should be. My brother and I made inquiries and discovered that you are the daughter of a great patriot, a man who fights against the Emperor, in Spain."

Louisa stared at her in amazement. "It is true my father is an officer," she answered, "and is at present taking part in the Peninsula campaign."

"May the English be successful," her companion murmured, very much as though it were a prayer. "Let me explain to you that my brother and I support the monarchy. We were only children during the revolution. Our father supported the king and lost his head on that account. Our mother fled with us to England. We were émigrés, among many others. We were raised here in a community of many others like us in Surrey. And we are committed, like so many others, to the return of the Bourbons to the throne."

This was another world than that inhabited by the Mrs. Thrashers of London, Louisa realized with a start. This was a world which she thought her father would not want her to ignore. And yet to take what was being said to her on face value might carry danger with it, although that was difficult to imagine here in this quiet London square.

It was no revelation to her that there were many Frenchmen still here in this country who did not support Napoleon, many who had not returned to their native country when they were free to do so

14

because they mistrusted the intentions of the arrogant Corsican who had used the army to take control of a country weakened almost to death by a bloody revolution followed by great confusion. And their resolve had hardened when it became clear that this same Corsican intended to make himself emperor not just of France, but of all of Europe perhaps including England as well.

"Very well," she said now, determined to be careful. "You believe you can trust me because of my father. I will accept that as a possibility. But trust me with what? With the fact that you and your brother are spies against the French? Why in the world should you have told me that?"

Her companion pushed back her bonnet a little, and Louisa saw more of her fine-boned face. Yes, she was very lovely, but there was a hard look in her green eyes which must give everyone who knew her pause. Louisa had no difficulty in believing that here was a woman dedicated to a cause.

"Let me continue a little longer to give you background," Mademoiselle Rioux told her. "It is necessary, I believe, in this situation. Our father died, as I told you. Our mother lives still, but she is an invalid. However, our home is still a center for—what do you call it—activities of a pro-Bourbon nature."

Louisa marveled at the chance this Frenchwoman was taking. Was this, in fact, a frank confession? If so, she thought it most unwise. Or was it some trick to involve her father indirectly. For the second time she warned herself to be careful.

"We have word from time to time of people who, although English, are secretly involved in helping Bonaparte for their own reasons," Mademoiselle Rioux continued. "Mercenary reasons, for the most part. People who are ready to pretend to be *en rapport* with the *haut ton*, but who, in actuality, use their position to gather information about English activities which would be of interest to the Emperor."

"I have never heard of such a thing!" Louisa gasped. "Surely my father would have mentioned . . ."

"Does he confide in you to that extent?" her companion demanded. And Louisa was forced to admit that he did not.

"Ask him, when you next meet, whether what I say is true or not," Mademoiselle Rioux challenged her. "Voilà! I challenge you to do so."

Louisa drew a breath and waited. This would be the test then. Did this stranger wish to quiz her about her father? If there was even a sign that she was intent on gathering information, she would rise and leave the square at once.

But her companion did nothing of the kind. Indeed, she seemed far more intent on making disclosures than receiving them.

"You were chosen quite deliberately by others besides my brother and myself to be of some help to our cause if you are agreeable," she told the girl, her blue eyes intent. "That is why we moved into the next house a few weeks ago, why I am meeting you here now in the open air. Where no one can hear us, you understand."

Louisa found it made her singularly uncomfortable to think that some people she did not know had chosen to keep watch over her activities. But still she decided she would listen. If what Mademoiselle Rioux was saying was true, her father would want her to listen. Looking across the square she saw that the brother had not changed his position. There was such an air of waiting about him that she shivered.

"It is Claude's *idée fixe* that these English men and women who support the Corsican will be caught," Mademoiselle Riouz said, following her glance. "I am committed, but he is even more so. Our father's death . . . But I have told you. Surely you will understand. If your own father had lost his head under the guillotine, you would want to continue to support the cause for which he died. He supported the Bourbons. We do the same. It is as simple as that."

Louisa did not think all this was simple, at all, but she did not say so. Instead she asked why it was thought that she could be of help.

"It is known that certain people whom you will shortly meet may very well be involved in passing secret information to the enemy. To Napoleon and all he represents. There, I have put it very simply, Mademoiselle Rogers. We have found it difficult to obtain access to that circle, for various reasons which will not interest you. When it was discovered that Captain Roger's daughter was to enter society, it was decided that we should try to enter with you. In a word, if you and I are friends—my brother Claude, as well, of course—then an *impasse* has been overcome. We will need nothing further from you. Only entry into a particular circle."

Louisa found that once again she did not know what to say. Should she put this woman off? Say that she must consider such a serious matter and then write to her father for advice? But it would be weeks before a letter would reach him, weeks again before he could reply. She could simply refuse and walk away from this. But what if she did and, learning of it later, her father should feel that she had failed to help the cause for which he risked his life? And if she gambled . . . If she believed them . . .

"What will happen to these persons if you are able to gather facts about them?" she demanded. "Facts which do indeed indicate that they gather English secrets and spread them about where they will do the greatest harm? What if some of these persons are people who befriend me?"

"If they are who we suspect," the stranger told her, "they are not people you would make your friends. Acquaintances, yes. But never friends. Unless I am greatly mistaken in your character."

"My character!" Louisa cried, jumping to her feet. "But you know nothing of it. Not really, Mademoiselle Rioux. The fact that I am my father's daughter means very little in reality. I may be attracted to the basest sorts."

The Frenchwoman laughed at that. She threw back her head, and her laughter was like the sound of bells. For some reason Louisa could never understand later, that laughter quite disarmed her. Suddenly she believed everything Mademoiselle Rioux had told her. And she decided to help her if she liked.

"Very well," the girl replied. "I will perform a few introductions. But I cannot do that until I have met people. Tonight Lady Landor and I go to a ball at Almack's. I will let you know whom I meet, and then you can decide if I will be any help."

The laughter might as well have been a signal, for she saw that the brother was coming toward them. He was dark, like his sister, and had the same intense blue eyes. Being introduced, he kissed Louisa's hand in the continental manner and murmured that he was pleased she had agreed to help them.

"I thought it possible, mademoiselle," he said, "you would not believe my sister. But I assure you that every word she has said to you is true. And there is no danger. Not for you or for anyone."

"But what about the people you uncover?" Louisa demanded.

"That will be the extent of it," he assured her, his eyes never wavering. Indeed, there was something even more about him than his sister which gave her confidence that she had made the right decision. "They will be exposed. Proof provided. Your own government can take appropriate action. We have connections, you see. Indeed, we work with your government very closely indeed."

She believed him. She believed them both. But just at the last moment, just before they parted, Louisa thought of something.

"Lady Landor is not involved in all of this, I take it," she asked them.

"You have my most sincere assurances that she is not," the brother told her. "Her affairs and ours are quite separate. Our paths will never meet except incidentally."

And with that they took leave of one another, having agreed to meet again after the ball at Almack's.

Chapter Three

THE assembly hall called Almack's was on King Street and, just before a ball, the neighborhood was crowded with carriages of every sort and description, from lozenged coaches to curricles to phaetons, all of them jockeying for position in the narrow street.

"I am so glad I took out a subscription," Lady Landor declared as she and Louisa waited in their carriage to approach the front door of the place. "We are certain to meet all sorts of interesting people if we make ourselves agreeable. I only hope my dress is not too casual. Living on the Continent, one gets out of touch."

Louisa guessed that she was nervous. For that matter, so was she. So much depended on this evening. Either Lady Landor would be snubbed quite publicly as Mrs. Thrasher had predicted, or she would not. In the first instance, it would be a great cruelty, for she, unlike Louisa, appeared to have had no warning. Perhaps she should have told her what Mrs. Thrasher had said, the girl thought now, as a silence fell between them. They were quite close to the assembly hall, and the faint sound of music could be heard in the soft, night air, blending with the voices of friends calling to one another. It was an atmosphere of close acquaintance which they might not be allowed to enter.

"I confess it is a mystery to me that we have had no invitations," Lady Landor had confided to Louisa that afternoon over tea.

They had been sitting in her little sitting room, a pleasant chamber, adjoining her boudoir. Through the window they could look across the square at the other stately houses. The sun had slid down far enough to shine directly into the room, matting the Oriental carpeting with gold and drawing thick fingers through the rich red of Lady Landor's hair.

"Have you no family?" Louisa had asked her, hoping to turn the awkward subject sideways to allow them to continue in a new

direction. Her conversation with Mrs. Thrasher had disturbed her
more than she had cared, at first, to admit, and, despite the difference in their age, Louisa was beginning to feel surprisingly protective of this strange, delightful creature.

"There is a cousin in Yorkshire, and an aunt in Devon," Lady
Landor continued thoughtfully, sipping her tea. In the oval glass
with the gilt frame hanging on the wall opposite, Louisa could see
the reflected contrast of them, her companion's exotic beauty
overblown and herself a slim study in black and white.

"And the Duke's family?" Louisa asked her.

Lady Landor laughed her deep laugh and threw back her head.
"Oh, but my dear, they have quite rejected me all these many
years. My blood was not rich enough. I had no *family*, or what
they meant by family. And I was so much younger. I expect they
did not even believe that I was fond of him."

"And were you?" Louisa murmured, thinking of how high
Miss Patterson would raise her eyebrows if she could overhear this
conversation.

"Oh, I was fond," Lady Landor told her, finishing her tea.
"But it was so dreadfully boring, you see. The Duke preferred everything about him to be Italian except me. And, as I said, I have
no head for language. Oh, how they chattered. It was like living in
an aviary! But he was always kind. And when letters came from
his sister, he would tear them straight across without reading them.
He did that for me."

So, Louisa thought, there was a sister who had opposed the
marriage. Was it possible that it was she who had spread the rumors about Lady Landor? Further questions elicited the fact that
the sister, Lady Ellis, did indeed live in London with her three
grown daughters, Patience, Fanny, and Horatia, spinsters all.

"I did not expect an invitation from them," Lady Landor
mused. "Or from their friends, in any case. No matter! We are going to Almack's this evening. We will easily make social contacts
there."

And, with that, she rang for Maria, her Italian maid, a personage who seemed to find England a dismal place, to judge from her
expression. She was very tall and narrow with a long, doleful face,
olive brown in color, and sad, black eyes. If she ever spoke,
whether in English or Italian, Louisa had never heard her. But she
appeared to suit Lady Landor to a T, for she could chat on to her
for hours without caring that she had no reply.

Louisa left them together, the abigail being informed as to which gown her mistress wished to wear and the fashion in which her hair would be done, afraid that, were she to remain, she would show something of her anxiety. If they were truly to go to Almack's, it would not be possible for Lady Landor to remain undeceived. The public snub was the worst sort Louisa could conceive, and, although she did not care on her own account, she could not bear to think how Lady Landor would respond.

And now they were about to take the plunge. Any excuse not to do so would only be a meaningless delay. Their footmen helped them from their carriage, and they joined the elegantly dressed company streaming up the stairs. Lady Landor took Louisa's hand of a sudden and squeezed it, and somehow the girl knew, despite the gloves they both were wearing, that the older woman's hands were cold.

Still, on the surface, Lady Landor showed nothing of any nervousness at all. Her pelisse was an extraordinary affair, for so many silver beads were sewn on it that it made her glitter when she walked. Underneath she wore a scarlet, satin gown cut low at the bodice and high at the hem to disclose charming ankles sheathed in pink-tinged stockings and high-heeled shoes that matched her gown. As for her chestnut hair, she had ignored the custom that a mature woman wear a turban at such events, and instead had had Maria wind it high on her head in great, chestnut coils, all decorated with pearls. Certainly she had not come to Almack's to be ignored.

Once again, aware of the contrast between them, Louisa stood beside Lady Landor when they entered the ballroom, hoping that, properly gowned as she was all in white muslin, with blue embroidery about the hem and bodice and with her black curls caught back in an undecorated chignon, she would serve to tame some of the flamboyance of her companion's appearance. Earlier, when Lady Landor was dressing, Louisa had tried to throw a few hints to the wind, professing to admire a more decorous lavender gown of satin which she found in the wardrobe.

"Oh, but my husband always liked to have me create a splash when we went out in public," Lady Landor had declared. "He married me for my beauty, or so he used to tell me, and it was my responsibility to make the most of it. Particularly," she added with a smile, "since I did not speak Italian."

21

Now, however, Louisa was certain that she had been wrong not to have insisted that Lady Landor moderate her taste. A cotillion was just ending as they came through the wide double doorway and, in an instant, or so it seemed, every eye in the ballroom was riveted on Lady Landor, who chose to take the attention as a compliment.

"La, child. See how they stare," she murmured behind the shelter of her fan. "And see them whisper! They will be asking who we are. You may be certain of it."

It was not highly likely, Louisa thought, that, given Lady Landor's ride that afternoon along The Mall, there were many members of the exclusive circle of the *haut ton* who did not know by now who this exotic creature beside her was. If there were whispers, they were not requests of identity, but rather the vehicle of sifting rumor. She felt a sudden chill but kept a smile on her face as she and Lady Landor made their way into the room.

"I confess to feeling awkward," the older woman said. "Everyone is looking at us, and yet no one comes forward with an introduction. Do you expect that we should simply choose someone and introduce ourselves? Your father meant to acquaint me with his friends, you know, although they are mostly bachelors who never stray far from their clubs. But there was no time, and I told him it did not matter. Now I wonder if I was wrong."

As she spoke, she smiled, but in a more fixed manner than before. As for Louisa, she felt the awkwardness as well and started when someone spoke her name.

"So you managed a subscription to Almack's, my dear," Mrs. Thrasher exclaimed. "Usually the sponsors are more particular in their decisions. Still, someone should have warned them, I expect."

Lady Landor either did not hear her clearly, or did not detect the slur. Her face lighted up even more brightly as she inclined her head in Mrs. Thrasher's direction.

"This must be the friend you joined this afternoon for a promenade," she said, apparently forgetting what Louisa had said when she had rejoined her in her carriage about Mrs. Thrasher being someone she would not want to know. Clearly the sheer relief of being spoken to by someone had excited her, for she seemed to tremble on the brink of the introduction she expected.

22

Louisa, however, had heard every word Mrs. Thrasher had said, and had taken the woman's meaning completely. She felt her face burning as she made her reply.

"Obviously the patrons cannot be too particular, madam," she replied, "if they allow you membership. And, by the by, I took the occasion this afternoon to write to Miss Patterson to describe something of our encounter. I do not think that she will ever trouble you again to welcome one of her little brood to London."

And, with that, she took Lady Landor by the arm and led her to one side, all too well aware that the encounter with Mrs. Thrasher had been watched by nearly everyone in the room and listened to by those who were nearest, with the result that the whispering campaign had now begun in earnest as everything that had been said was relayed across the room.

"My dear!" Lady Landor cried, taking Louisa's arm. "I cannot believe my ears. Why, you insulted her, you know. There can be no doubt about it. What in heaven's name possessed you? Oh, dear! I have just seen dear Alfred's sister! And are those her daughters with her? I have not seen them for years! Oh, my! Time has not improved them. Only look how they are staring in this direction. Do you think they can have seen me?"

Given the circumstances, Louisa did not know how it was possible that they had not seen Lady Landor, particularly since she was clearly the topic of conversation of everyone in the room. As for whom she was referring to, since Alfred had been her late husband's name, the ladies in question must be his sister and her daughters, Patience, Fanny, and Horatia.

Looking in the direction indicated by her companion, Louisa saw a gimlet-eyed personage who gave the general impression of a quill pen, being bone thin but with such giant feathers sticking in her turban as to make her seem distressingly top-heavy. Beside her stood three ladies, rather long in the tooth in that they had put their schooldays far behind them. Louisa recalled that Lady Landor had indicated they were, all three, unmarried, and, seeing them, she thought that came as no surprise. All three were dumpy as to figure. All three had complexions like a vanilla pudding which has set too long. But there *were* differences; one appeared to have a cast in her left eye which conveyed the disconcerting impression that she was looking in two directions at once. The second had teeth which splayed in all directions, and the third had a slanted nose. All in all they made a curious assortment, Louisa told her-self.

"Oh, dear, I did so hope I would not meet them," Lady Landor murmured. "At least not right away. Before Alfred married me, Lucasta said all manner of things about me. Of course, I am certain she was sorry after."

Somehow, watching the lady under discussion send piercing glances across the room, Louisa was quite certain that she had not been sorry. Indeed, it seemed quite probable that, given the fact that she had spread scandal before, she had been prepared to do the same again when she had heard that her brother's widow was to return to England.

Meanwhile, the heads of the assembled company were turning back and forth as they awaited, in concert, whatever developments might be forthcoming. There were, Louisa thought, three alternatives, only one of them pleasant and that the least likely, since Lady Ellis had made no effort to contact her sister-in-law since her return to London. Otherwise, she might ignore her, which would be the least awkward course, or there could be a confrontation.

"Perhaps it might be just as wise if we were to pretend we had not seen her," Louisa ventured. "The great thing is to avoid any unpleasantness."

"Oh, but she is coming across the floor to see me," Lady Landor exclaimed. "No doubt she wants to make it up. How astonished Alfred would be! Still, I can afford to forgive and forget. There is no harm in being generous."

It was true enough that Lady Ellis was coming in their direction, with her three daughters following. The crowd parted for them like the Red Sea, and a little hush fell on the assemblage. The musicians, who had been tuning up for a waltz, set their instruments aside and did not bother to hide their curiosity. Lady Landor smiled, but it was all too clear to Louisa what the outcome of this encounter would be. Glimpsing Mrs. Thrasher's face in the crowd, she shivered at the rapacious look in the eyes of someone who clearly relished what was to come.

And then, quite suddenly, just as Lady Ellis was approaching, a gentleman appeared. He was tall, with a commanding presence, and dark with eyes which seemed to glitter with some private rage. Whether intentionally or not, he placed himself between Lady Landor and her sister-in-law who, seeing him, came to an abrupt halt, with Patience, Fanny, and Horatia tumbling over her like dominoes.

"Lady Landor, I believe," the stranger said, making a bow. "And Miss Rogers. I know your father well. I am Miles Cardross."

"Oh, but of course!" Lady Landor declared. "You are a viscount, I believe, and you have an estate in Essex where Captain Rogers goes to hunt occasionally."

"Madam, you are correct in every detail," Lord Cardross said with a thin smile which did not match the expression in his eyes when Lady Ellis ventured to tap him on the arm with her fan.

"My mother has asked me to tell you that she would be pleased if you would sit with her," the viscount declared, ignoring Lady Ellis completely.

"How kind," Lady Landor cried. "But first I would have you meet my sister-in-law, Lady Ellis, and her daughters. We were about to make a reconciliation after all these years."

Lord Cardross's expected appearance had clearly disconcerted Lady Ellis, and she was making tutting noises under her breath, not very confidently.

"I am acquainted with Lady Ellis and her daughters," Lord Cardross said with a slight edge to his voice. "And I am certain that she will put off your reunion to gratify my mother's wish to make a conversation with you. Here. Will you take my arm? And Miss Rogers, too. They are about to play a waltz, I think. Perhaps after Lady Landor is settled, you would honor me by being my partner."

And, with his handsome face expressionless, he swept them off, leaving Lady Ellis and her daughters clearly speechless.

Chapter Four

"NO doubt you think I am precipitous, Miss Rogers," Lord Cardross said when they had finished the waltz and were standing in the alcove of a window, looking out at the London night. "I must have seemed to you to make an unnecessary interruption at the moment of a reunion, simply to carry you and Lady Landor away."

Louisa looked up at him with a glance which did not waver. The first time she had laid eyes on him, she had been struck most by the anger in his eyes. It was gone now, but an expression she could not interpret remained. Next, she had been impressed by the way he had taken command of the situation. His mother, a kind-faced woman with hair as white and soft as silk, had welcomed Lady Landor almost fondly, and spoken to both her and Louisa of her admiration for Captain Rogers. People were watching them. Louisa was very conscious of it, but neither Lord Cardross nor his mother took any heed, and Lady Landor was too puzzled and confused to notice. Clearly she was pleased at the attention. But she had been bewildered by the way she had been whisked away from Lady Ellis.

So, this gentleman was handsome and self-possessed. And there was mystery in his eyes. Clearly he was someone of importance, for when they waltzed, room was always made for them and looks were respectful. Louisa thought that she had never known before tonight that so much could be read from faces. The same eyes which had seemed to accuse Lady Landor and herself when they had made their entry had assumed quite another expression now. Some sort of victory had been won, although Louisa was not at all certain what it was and who had been defeated—unless, of course, it had been Lady Ellis, whom she had seen watching from the sidelines when she and the young viscount had swooped about the floor.

27

"There is no crime in being precipitous, sir," she told him now. "I will be frank with you and say that I think an awkward situation would have developed if you had not come when you did."

"You are perceptive, Miss Rogers," he replied, turning in just such a way as to throw his face into the shadows. "Tell me. Are you aware of the situation?"

Louisa paused. "You said, I think, you are a good friend of my father's."

"You heard Lady Landor say that she remembered his mentioning my name. What a pity he did not mention me to you, as well, since it seems I need credentials."

"I have no reason to disbelieve you," Louisa replied. "But I have reason to think that there are people in this city who would be glad enough to see Lady Landor embarrassed, and I intend to see that does not happen."

"Which means you must be careful whom you confide in."

Louisa smiled. "We understand one another," she murmured. "Very well, then, it is too late for you to beg off, sir. You have solicited my confidances, and you are about the receive them."

Lord Cardross made a low, mock bow. "The pleasure is mine, Miss Rogers," he declared.

"Yes," Louisa told him. "I expect you can think of nothing you would rather be doing than listening to the promises of a perfect stranger. Listen by all means, sir, but do not make a pretense of enjoying it."

"What pretenses I make are mine to choose," he told her, but he was smiling, too, marking his words as banter. "Let me repeat. Are you aware of the situation?"

At that, Louisa told him about her encounter with Mrs. Thrasher that afternoon. "She said all sorts of rumors were being circulated about Lady Landor," she declared indignantly. "She make it plain that, in her opinion, every door in London will be closed to her. Indeed, she wanted me to come away and live with her instead."

"Did you find that a temptation?" he asked her, turning back to face Louisa so that the glitter of the chandelier nearest them tranferred to his dark eyes.

"To stay with Mrs. Thrasher?" Louisa exclaimed. "Why, I would not so much as set foot in her drawing room, let alone become her guest."

"And so you refused her outright?" he said, and Louisa thought she noted a tone of amusement in his voice. No doubt he thought her singularly naïve. But, after all, what did that matter? He was a friend of her father, although years younger. He and his mother had been kind to her and Lady Landor. If he cared to find her amusing, let him! As for herself, she intended to be honest, if nothing else.

"I am afraid that I insulted her," she told him. "Certainly I was impertinent. And there was no question as to my rudeness when she accosted us as we came into the ballroom tonight. However, she deserved it. She must learn that I will not allow the lady my father is to marry to be insulted in any way."

The music was being struck again, this time for a gavotte. As though he did not wish to be interrupted, Lord Cardross made an impatient gesture and, taking Louisa's arm, moved her farther down the room, taking no notice when people turned to stare. As for Louisa, she tossed her dark curls and eyed them defiantly until she and Lord Cardross reached the sanctuary of another window alcove.

"You can see that it is a matter of some importance to me to see to it that you understand the situation," Lord Cardross told her, clearly oblivious of everything except their conversation. "When your father and Lady Landor arrived in London, I was away . . . No matter. I was away and could not warn him of what was bound to happen. Indeed, I would not have heard a word of it, since I have been deeply occupied in . . . other matters, had it not been for my mother. Oh yes. And my sister, too. There she is, dancing with Hugh Trever. The fair girl wearing blue."

"She and your mother knew how Lady Landor was to be treated?" Louisa asked him.

"They had been in the country and did not hear about what Lady Ellis had done until they returned to London yesterday. This has been the first occasion we have had to make a public demonstration that the lady that your father has chosen to be his wife will be received by us."

Involuntarily, Louisa took his hand and thanked him. "But what is it precisely that Lady Ellis has done to mark Lady Landor's character?" she asked him. "Nothing you can say will shock me. That must be understood. All that Mrs. Thrasher would say is that Lady Landor is a flirt. And when I told her that I did not think that a novelty, she said that she had married for wealth."

"That much is true, I understand."

"She makes no secret of it," Louisa told him. "She married young and at her family's command. Even today she only thinks of how she pleased them. And pleased the Duke, as well. She is a simple creature in many ways. And she seems to love my father. That much is certain. As far as I am concerned, sir, that is all that matters."

She broke off, flushing, as she saw how closely Lord Cardross was looking at her. "You are very like your father in many ways, Miss Rogers," he said in a low voice which she could barely hear over the music. "Loyalty is a virtue which he prizes, as well. Of course you have not had the opportunity to hear from him since he returned to Spain, but . . ."

"My dear Miles," a woman's voice declared. "How clever of you to have foiled that frightful Lady Ellis! I saw it all, and, I assure you, you have my congratulations. This is Miss Rogers, isn't it? At least that is what everyone says."

The speaker was a wiry little woman of middle age with darting sparrow's eyes and a brisk manner.

"I am the Duchess of Taxton, my dear," she said by way of introduction. "The proper reference is Your Grace, but in prolonged conversations, such as this, you may say madam. An unnecessary explanation, no doubt, but people are so lax today about forms of address that I find it is best to establish certain guide lines. My husband says that it is rude, but I have never minded a bit of rudeness if my purpose can be accomplished. Now, what is it you are discussing? I hope it is the malice which has been spread about Lady Landor. What an unusual woman she is in appearance! Quite beautiful, of course, in an exotic way. It will go against her, you know, if she continues to be flamboyant. Quite unfair, of course, but there it is. It will only make people more willing to believe everything Lady Ellis is saying."

"And precisely what is that, madam?" Louisa said, resisting the urge to drown in the torrent of the duchess's words. Clearly she was someone who always spoke to the point and took little time for pleasantries other than establishing precisely what it was she should be called.

The duchess looked at her approvingly. "I like directness, gel," she said. "And I will answer in kind. Lady Ellis claims that her sister-in-law was consistantly involved in one flirtation after another, all the years she lived in Florence. She claims her brother was made most unhappy by her and that his demands that she act in a less giddy manner were met with blunt refusals. Lady Ellis says that Lady Landor made her brother's dying days a misery and that, after his death, she lost no time in making new acquaintances, without a proper mourning period. There are other charges, but those, I think, are too absurd to consider.''

Having said this, she looked back and forth from Louisa to Lord Cardross in a speculative way, as though inordinately interested in their response.

"Where did she get her information?'' Louisa demanded. "Had she spies in Florence, I wonder. How vicious of her! Even worse, people are prepared to believe her.''

"Not everyone,'' Lord Cardross observed, his dark eyes intent on her face.

"It is a great thing that you have the support of the Cardross family,'' the duchess murmured behind her fan. "They constitute a social power which Lady Ellis would do well not to underestimate.''

Remembering the way Lady Ellis had looked at the young viscount when he had come between her and Lady Landor, Louisa thought that this was probably quite true. But she had seen the cruel look in that same lady's eyes, and she thought that not even the patronage of the Cardross family, welcome as it was, would halt her storm of abuse.

"I intend to speak to her in private,'' Louisa said in a low voice. "To Lady Ellis, I mean. This—this abuse of Lady Landor cannot be allowed to go on.''

The duchess cocked her head and looked at the girl from a different angle. "You may be young, my dear,'' she said in her crisp voice, "but you have a sure supply of confidence, I see.''

"Determination, madam,'' Louisa replied.

"Then I must warn you that a visit to that woman and her daughters will be like voluntarily going into a bed of snakes.''

Louisa reflected that the duchess was nothing if not forthright. And yet she could think of nothing more to the point than to put a halt to the rumors Lady Ellis had been spreading out of sheer frustrated malice and nothing else. She had been opposed to her brother's marriage all those many years ago. And she had allowed her fury to fester until it had broken out like a great sore. Of one thing Louisa was certain. She would not allow either herself or Lady Landor to be infected.

"Do you want me to go with you?" Lord Cardross said. "I can tell from your expression that you will not allow yourself to be dissuaded, Miss Rogers, and it might be that, as your father's friend, I could lend considerable support."

"Come, Miles," the duchess said, laughing. "You would have no patience with a women's quarrel. I had much better accompany you, Miss Rogers."

"Thank you both," Louisa replied. "But this is something that I must attempt myself."

"Nothing will work with that woman except threats, my dear," the duchess told her. "And I cannot think how you . . ."

"I would not underestimate Miss Rogers, madam," Lord Cardross told her. "Indeed, I think she is even more like her father than I first thought."

Chapter Five

THE next morning, however, on her return from her visit to Lady Ellis, Louisa was convinced that Lord Cardross had compared her to her father far too readily. Her cheeks stung with the anger she still felt when she thought of the way she had been greeted, and she bit her lower lip in irritation as she descended from the carriage, not much relishing going up to her bed chamber to brood over what had happened. As a result, when she saw Mademoiselle Rioux standing at one of the long windows of the next house and gesturing, Louisa felt relief.

The sudden whirlwind of affairs which had begun the other night at Almack's had kept her from thinking of the strange interview in the square with the improbable *agent provocateur* and her dour brother. Now, remembering the promise she had made them, Louisa found she was not sorry. They would, at least, provide her with a welcome distraction from Lady Landor's affairs.

And so it was she smiled her acceptance and hurried up the flight of stone stairs of the house next door, wondering as she did so if it had been assumed by the young French couple that she would keep her association with them secret from Lady Landor and the servants in her household. But surely not. After all, she was to introduce them as friends. Keep everything as simple as possible. Say that they had met in the square, which was as true as anything could be. Say that they were neighbors, another fact in point. She determined not to make any foolish nonsense of this, *not* to play spies and dangers. They only wanted introductions from her and that was all she would provide.

And yet, she wondered, as she waited at the door, if it might not be that they had been wrong about the people she would meet. Certainly she could not think of anyone she had encountered at Almack's who might possibly be a spy for such a gentleman as Napoleon had proved himself to be. It could hardly be Lady Ellis or her daughters, even though it was a pity. After what had happened this morning, Louisa would have liked Lady Ellis to be one of the people mademoiselle and her brother meant to expose.

As for the others, Louisa scarcely thought that Mrs. Thrasher, given the looseness of her lips, could be a spy. As for the Duchess of Taxton, she knew very little of her. And the only other person she had met had been Lord Cardross, a friend of her father and . . .

"Bonjour, mon ami!" Mademoiselle Rioux announced, throwing open the door. "You must forgive me for making you wait, but I had to come myself since we keep very few servants, being here on such a temporary basis, you understand. *Entrez vous* and welcome! Come into the sitting room just here. Let me take your shawl. You will not mind being informal. Voilà! There is no help for it. You remember my brother."

Once again Monsieur Rioux kissed her fingers fleetingly. His blue eyes were as intense as they had been the afternoon before, and Louisa remembered what his sister had said about his obsession. Somehow the thought chilled her and she shivered, causing her youthful hostess to draw her near the fire and recommend a chair.

"It is such a damp and dreary morning," she announced. "I will ask Estelle to bring us some hot chocolate."

Louisa watched her sweep out of the room, a slim figure in a simple but elegant morning dress of the finest muslin. Her dark hair was covered with a large mobcap, but even this she managed to endow with style and, as she turned at the door to smile and recommend that her brother make himself agreeable, Louisa saw that her impression of the other day had been correct. Mademoiselle Rioux was very beautiful.

As soon as she had left, however, Louisa felt uncomfortable. Apparently as far as Monsieur Rioux was concerned, silence was his forte. Avoiding his stony gaze, Louisa looked about the room, noticing that it was as sparcely furnished as might indicate a temporary stay, but that it was comfortable enough with its three wing chairs and a Sheraton settee, not to mention a few landscape paintings on the white paneled walls. There was an Adam fireplace with wreaths and molded scrolls and an Aixminster rug on the floor. Having noted all these details, Louisa took a deep breath and tried to launch a conversation.

It was anything but a success. The gentleman admitted that the

34

weather had been beastly—*malheur*, he said—and that property in London was difficult to rent. And then, since he so clearly was not bent on a tête-à-tête until his sister returned, Louisa settled back in her big chair and considered the events of the morning, promising herself that she would think of them once and then put them out of her mind entirely.

Somehow, in her own drawing room, Lady Ellis had not looked quite so much like a quill pen, partly because she was wearing a morning cap instead of feathers and partly because she had not had her daughters with her, at least not at first. Sweeping through the double doorway, the taffeta skirts of her gown crackling round her, she had declared in a sharp voice that Louisa had taken her by surprise.

"We have not been formally introduced, Miss Rogers," she had said in a voice which squeaked at the edges like chalk on slate. "But I am completely aware of who you are and your relationship with my sister-in-law. I cannot think what business you may have with me."

"Your treatment of Lady Landor is my business, madam," Louisa had replied in a determined fashion. "I believe that you are responsible for the falsehoods spread about her, and I have come to ask you to retract them."

What a fool she had been, Louisa thought now as she stared into the fire, to have thought that anything could be accomplished in so direct a way. No doubt Lady Ellis had thought herself quite right to have called her visitor insolent and a chit of a girl, scarely out of the schoolroom. There had been more in the same line, a perfect torrent of it, about how she could see that Mrs. Thrasher's first impressions had been right and that Louisa was, indeed, an impudent jade.

"Mrs. Thrasher has written a letter to your headmistress, my girl," Lady Ellis had told her. "I should not be a bit surprised if you do not hear from that quarter immediately."

Louisa's eyes had not wavered for a minute. She could remember that, at least, with pride. "Miss Patterson will have heard from me as well by now," she had informed the lady. "And, unless I am mistaken, she will treat Mrs. Thrasher's report of the incident for precisely what it is worth. Furthermore, much as I admire my headmistress, I am no longer in her charge, nor ever will be again."

That was the closest she had come to victory, for Lady Ellis had rapidly launched into an attack on Louisa's father whom she said must be completely besotted to have given her over to the care of "that dreadful woman." On and on she had gone, not giving Louisa a chance to respond. Indeed, the only thing needed to cool her rage had been the arrival of her three daughters who had trooped into the room to the accompaniment of whispers and giggles which would have better suited ladies half their age.

Only then had Lady Ellis reversed her tone from one of anger to appeal as she stressed Patience's skill on the pianoforte, Fanny's proficiency with needlework, and Horatia's soprano voice. She added that Louisa would be wise to abandon her present hostess and come to stay with them, adding that further acquaintance with her daughters was sure to be beneficial to her.

At that, Patience had fixed Louisa firmly with her cross eye, while looking at her mother with the other, and Fanny had bared her teeth in a rather frightful smile. As for Horatia, she had twitched her sideways-slanted nose, and Louisa had decided it was time to beat retreat.

What an odd world it was, she decided. One minute she had been having harsh words with a lady she had never met until the evening before, and now she was waiting to be served chocolate by a French spy. Miss Patterson had tried to prepare her for London, but she had not suggested anything as extraordinary as this.

Mademoiselle Rioux appeared in the doorway at just that moment, burdened with a large silver tray. Quickly Louisa went to help her, and somehow, in the process of setting everything out on a marble-topped table, she felt as though she were with a friend. Apparently Mademoiselle Rioux had the same feeling, for as she handed her brother his cup and saucer, she suggested in her low sweet-accented voice that she and Louisa use their Christian names with one another.

"I am Michelle," she said. "And my brother's name is Claude. I know that it is not customary for young English ladies to refer to gentlemen informally. You must please yourself. Whatever you call him, he does not mind. As I told you yesterday, he thinks of nothing but revenge on those who would betray our country. And that is *comme il faut*, do you not agree?"

"Perhaps it *is* to be expected," Louisa said hesitantly. "It certainly does not seem to make him happy."

She broke off realizing that she might have committed a *faux pas*, as no doubt Michelle would call it, in making such an intimate reference to the state of Monsieur Rioux's mind, but neither sister nor brother appeared to take offense.

"Now," Michelle said, taking a seat very close to Louisa, "you must tell us all about it. The entertainment at Almack's, I mean. We saw you leaving the house last night *en grande tenue*. Even Claude agreed that you looked very beautiful."

Claude gave his sister an even more dour look than usual, but did not grace her with an answer. "The question is, whom did she meet," he muttered, almost as though Louisa were not in the room at all.

"He wants me to get down to business, as you English put it," Michelle murmured. "Claude was never one for chitchat."

"I quite understand," Louisa replied, sipping her chocolate which was very rich indeed. "I really doubt that anyone I met last night is the sort of person to arouse your interest."

Claude indicated that he and his sister would be the ones to decide that, and, although it was charmingly said, there was an undercurrent to his voice that made Louisa uneasy.

"You must not mind him," Michelle murmured. "He is all eagerness, you understand. He has never been patient. He thinks of these people we are to find as those who have been guilty of *lèse-majesté*. As you say, high treason."

"I do not think that I am to move in as exhaulted circles as you may have been led to believe," Louisa told them. "At Almack's we encountered a Mrs. Thrasher, whom I have met before. She seems a perfectly ordinary woman, much engaged in gossip."

"Gossips are sometimes the best people for the sort of thing we are trying to track down," Michelle assured her. They are apt to be *au courant* with everything which is going on. Ah, but Claude is shaking his head. I see your Mrs. Thrasher is not on our list."

Louisa turned to see that, indeed, Claude had a piece of foolscap in his hand. On it she could see a list of names, and it seemed to her that the list was rather long. Surely there could not be that many people in London, or even in all of England, intent on support of Boney, as he was called by the irreverent.

"Who else was there, Miss Rogers, *s'il vous plaît?*" the intent gentleman declared with an undercurrent of urgency in his voice which reminded Louisa that, to him at least, this was the most serious business in the world.

"There was a Lady Ellis and her daughters," Louisa told him. "I had occasion to see her again this morning. She is sister-in-law to the lady I live with, but other than that she has little to recommend her. Indeed, I have not met a more unpleasant person in all my life."

"Is she mentioned, Claude?" Michelle demanded.

He raised his dark hair and stared at her intently. "I do not think that is anything Miss Rogers wishes to know," he told her. "I may have shaken my head over Mrs. Thrasher, but that means nothing. Nothing. Who may or may not be on this list is *de trop* as far as Miss Rogers is concerned. It is not her affair."

His French accent was thicker than his sister's, and he spoke so rapidly that Louisa was not certain she had heard him correctly. At least not every word. But she agreed with the general theme, and so she told them.

"I have agreed to help you in a very particular way," she said. "I will tell you whom I meet and, if you like, introduce you. But you are quite correct, monsieur. It would be better if that were the extent of my involvement."

Monsieur Rioux looked at her with approval, and Michelle smiled. "No doubt it will be better so," she murmured. "Whom else did you meet? It does not seem so far that it was a very exciting evening.

It took Louisa by surprise to reflect that that was the way it must sound, indeed. And yet she had not thought of it as boring. Indeed, quite the contrary.

"There was the Duchess of Taxton," she added. "And Lady Cardross. And her son. His name, I think, is Miles."

She had been looking off into the middle distance as she recited these names, but she did not miss the glance which flew between Michelle and her brother. What did it mean, that look, she wondered? Which one of the names she had just recited had they recognized? Or had they recognized them all?

"Anyone else?" Claude demanded. "I think you may be a great help to us, Miss Rogers."

Louisa frowned. "There *is* someone, but I have not met him yet. His name is Sir Thomas Tigger, and he is a world traveler. At least he has made many visits to Florence. Lady Ellis spoke of him to me just before I left her house this morning, and I believe she will arrange to have him contact me about—about a certain matter."

She closed her eyes for a moment, recollecting the last confrontation with Lady Ellis. "I can provide you with an eyewitness to my sister-in-law's behavior while she lived in Florence," Lady Ellis had said with the satisfaction of one who feels she has played her cards to the best possible advantage. "Someone who has had occasion to observe her closely. Sir Thomas Tigger is a great traveler, and every time he goes abroad he stays in Florence. But perhaps you are afraid to talk to him directly for fear of hearing something you do not wish to hear."

Remembering how she had assured the woman that she was not afraid of hearing anyone speak on that topic or any other, Louisa flushed.

"Is anything the trouble?" Michelle asked her, putting down her cup and saucer to move closer. "Has anything we have said distressed you?"

"I have distressed myself," Louisa said with a little laugh. "Earlier this morning. But that is of no account as far as you are concerned. I must go now. I have mentioned everyone I can think of. My circle does not promise to be as extensive as it might have been because . . . But, again, that does not matter. I hope I have been of some help to you."

"Ah, but you have been, I assure you!" Claude exclaimed, rising as she did, his charming manners returning. "Indeed, my sister and I would be well pleased if an occasion arises in the near future when you are to see any one of the people you just mentioned with the exception of Mrs. Thrasher."

"Do you mean that all of them are on your list?" Louisa exclaimed.

"No, Miss Rogers," the French gentleman said very seriously indeed. "I do not mean that at all. Remember that you put a limit to the extent you wished to be involved. Only remember that if one or a number of them . . ."

"I will arrange it if I can do so," Louisa told him. "But, as I said, my social situation is uncertain. It may be that I will never see any of them again."

Chapter Six

LOUISA soon discovered, however, that she was not to be neglected as she had feared she might be. Returning home, she found Lady Landor, magnificent in dishabille, waiting for her in a joyous mood.

"We have received our first invitation," she exclaimed, waving a bit of paper in the air. "From Lady Cardross. It is to be a small, private party at their house in Albemarle Street. How exciting that will be!"

Louisa reflected that she should take a moment and write a note to Michelle, telling her the promising news. And then, as she watched Lady Landor dance around the room, her next thought was that it should be herself whirling about and not the older woman. In some strange way their situations were reversed. And yet, if one thought on it, it was not so difficult to understand. Her companion may have moved in the best Florentine society but, at her own admission, she had not really been a part of it because of her inability to speak the language. It might have been, as well, that her father's friends had all been a good deal older than she. Perhaps this invitation was the first to give her pleasure in many years.

That was one side of the coin. But even as she assured Lady Landor that she was delighted and began a discussion of what they were to wear, one part of Louisa's mind remembered what Lady Ellis had said. It was all very well to tell herself that the woman was as insidious as the Duchess of Taxton had warned her she would be. But it still stung her that the woman had implied that she, Louisa, would not want to see Sir Thomas Tigger because she did not want to know the truth. Well, Louisa told herself now, she would show Lady Ellis she was wrong. After all, she had another motive now to meet as many members of the *haut ton* as she could. Even the names she had mentioned to Michelle and her brother this morning had seemed to interest them. And, she remembered now, Sir Thomas Tigger's name had been among them.

But that was something she could not allow herself to speculate about. This was something in which she would not really be involved, except to provide whatever introductions she could. Lady Landor was her first consideration and now, watching Maria hold up first one gown and then another from her companion's extensive wardrobe, Louisa told herself to dismiss any doubts which might have crept into her mind. Her father had chosen this woman. Her own acquaintance with her had disclosed nothing except a childlike goodness. Perhaps she was frivolous. Perhaps she liked to be admired. What beautiful woman did not. And the mere fact that she was lavish in everything she did and that she dressed in a flamboyant manner should not disturb. The stories Lady Ellis had spread were born of malice, nothing else. And if this gentleman named Tigger were to claim that they were true, then he was nothing more than her confederate in the attempt to blacken Lady Landor's name.

And so, although she could not help being troubled, Louisa tried to match Lady Landor's enthusiasm for the evening ahead. Their preparations served as an excuse not to go riding on The Mall. Louisa knew that, whatever else she did, she must keep Lady Landor from appearing in public in such a way as to give credence to the rumors that were being circulated. There was very little she could do directly, short of telling her companion the truth, as was proved when she encouraged her to wear a modest gown of soft, gray silk.

"Why, dear child, I couldn't possibly!" Lady Landor exclaimed. "That is my sad dress, and it would not be at all appropriate to wear it on such a happy occasion as our real debut in London society."

Further explanation followed, to the effect that often, in Florence, she had been unhappy. Bright colors always served to raise her spirits. Or nearly always.

"If I found myself telling Maria to take this dress out of the wardrobe," she explained to Louisa, running a brush through her thick, chestnut curls, "I knew that I must take drastic measures to put myself in a good humor again."

Louisa was standing behind her as she sat at her dressing table, and their eyes met in the glass. Only when put in contrast with Louisa's youthful flow, did Lady Landor seem overripe. Louisa saw it, without any particular satisfaction. If Lady Landor noticed, she made no sign. Indeed, she reached up and pulled the girl's face down beside her own.

Although she laughed, Louisa was thinking troubled thoughts about what Lady Landor had just said. What drastic measures succeeded in putting her in good humor? Did she dare to ask? And she knew that if it had not been for Lady Ellis, she would not be asking herself these questions. That was the very worst of it. She had gone out this morning, full of confidence that she would put that woman in her place. Instead she had allowed her to plant suspicions in her own mind.

"What were those drastic measures?" she heard herself say, and wished that she did not dread the reply, wished that she was not watching Lady Landor so closely, watching for some sign of prevarication. But she asked the question because she had to, as much as to prove to herself that she could as anything else.

Now, to her consternation, Lady Landor made a pause. Indeed, she dropped her handkerchief, and Louisa was certain it was done with deliberation. She bent to help Lady Landor grope for it, only to have the woman turn her face away. And worse, when rising, Louisa saw that Maria seemed equally disconcerted. At least she was putting dresses back in the wardrobe in a strange, hurried sort of way. And her face was turned away, as well.

"Do you think that I should wear jewelry, my dear?" Lady Landor said, rising, slightly breathless from her search, with her handkerchief in her hand. "You know that it became unpopular during the revolution in France. No one wanted to be pointed out as an aristocrat, you see. At least that is what Alfred told me. The mode then spread to England and elsewhere, as French fashion always will. I only tell you this to explain that, as a consequence, I do not have as many pieces as I might have. But I do think, perhaps, the pearls . . ."

With that, the sentence dwindled out, and promptly she and Maria went in search of the aforementioned baubles, both of them with such a self-conscious air that Louisa made an excuse and left them to go to her own room.

The day dragged to its conclusion. For the first time since she had come to London, Louisa was conscious of a certain lack of confidence. How foolhearty she had been to come straight from the classroom to the city and think that she would instinctively know the ins and outs of things. Granted that Lord Cardross and his mother were the first agreeable people she had met, and they had taken Lady Landor on the basis of her father's recommendation. If he loved her, they would accept her. It was as simple as that. Then why, Louisa asked herself, could she not do the same? Without any hidden doubts?

But why, oh why, had Lady Landor been so disconcerted when she had asked a simple question? It must have been very lonely for her there in Florence, burdened by an aging husband and with no one at all to talk to, except Maria. She must have taken out the "sad dress" more than Louisa liked to think. Who could blame her for wanting desperately to raise her spirits? But what were those drastic measures? Lady Ellis would not hesitate to name them, Louisa thought. These worries and others troubled her so much that she could not think of the pleasures of the evening and lingered over her toilette, glad enough that she had refused Lady Landor's offer of an abigail so that she could be alone with herself and her thoughts.

When it was time, she joined Lady Landor in the corridor downstairs. There was a little awkwardness, but both of them hurried to smooth it over with a smile. Each complimented the other on how she was dressed to help to clear the air as much as for any other reason. And, indeed, there was room for compliments, for Louisa, despite her worries, glowed in a charming pale primrose gown, the bodice and the hem of which were trimmed with matching ribbon. She wore no decoration and her long gloves were plain, all of which provided no distraction from her lovely face with those intense blue eyes, eyes that lingered on Lady Landor.

And, indeed, the older woman was as prime to be looked at as a gallery of art. Her cheeks were more flushed than usual, and Louisa found herself suspecting the use of vermillion. At once she rebuked herself. What if Lady Landor aided nature. The majority of older women did. So would she in time, no doubt. And, as for the fact that the bodice of her companion's scarlet and silver striped gown was low, that was, after all, the fashion. At least she had not gone as far as Parisians were said to go, wetting themselves all over when they were dressed, in order to make the stuff the gown was made of stick more closely to their forms. And, if the feathers in the chestnut hair were arranged provocatively, it must be remembered that Lady Landor had been taught, ever since she was a little girl, to be no more than an ornament, first for her father's household and then for her husband's.

And so they traveled to Albemarle Street near Piccadilly, trying to bridge the strain between them by the pointing out of sights—a wagon with one wheel off, children playing at the side of such a busy street that the little smocked figures with their dirty hands and faces had learned to dart between the horses' feet, a dandy on his way to White's with his elaborately tied cravat and his hair cut in the Brutus fashion.

It was a relief, Louisa found, to reach their destination and be absorbed into the company. Resolving to forget her suspicions, the girl greeted Lady Cardross with a smile and was introduced to the fair-haired girl she had seen dancing the gavotte the night before. Beside her was her erstwhile partner, a good-looking gentleman with finely drawn features and laughing eyes.

"This is my daughter, Claire," Lady Cardross said, "and Mr. Hugh Trever, her fiancé. They are to be married in the autumn."

"I hope we can be friends," Claire Cardross said, taking Louisa's hand. "I am so fond of your papa. Although we hardly ever see him now that Wellington is fighting the French in Spain."

"Has he ever explained to you exactly what his duties are, Miss Rogers?" Mr. Trever said. "I've laid the groundwork for him to tell me by casting out hints as thick and fast as I dare. But that is one thing he is close of mouth about."

"No doubt for a good reason," Lord Cardross declared. He had come up behind Louisa with little warning, and she gave a start which subsequently made her flush when she looked at him. He was quite as handsome as she remembered him, and his dark eyes were just as searching. However, Louisa was a practical girl, and she reminded herself that he was not looking at her in any different fashion, as far as she could see, than the way he had looked at Lady Landor when he had greeted her a few minutes before. How full of fancies her mind seemed to be ever since she had come to London. In time, no doubt, she would be herself again, and in the meantime she resolved to be, above all else, as practical as she could be.

"Do you think the Captain carries messages from Wellington to the government?" Hugh was demanding. "Come, Miles, I'll swear that you know more about it that you are saying. Perhaps your father reports to the Prince Regent, Miss Rogers, because . . ."

"In wartime, it is just as well not to speculate about what any-one does," Lord Cardross suggested. "Besides, there must be an-other subject we could just as well pursue."

"There is one thing I want to mention before Mama and Lady Landor join us," Claire said in a low voice. "Am I correct in say-ing that Lady Landor knows nothing of what is being said about her? Mama said that, of course, she did not mention it last night. But Miles said that you knew about all the slander, Miss Rogers. The thing is, we want to know how careful we should be about what we say."

"She knows nothing," Louisa said, with a glance over her shoulder. "And I would like so much to keep it just that way. I in-tend to find a way of stopping Lady Ellis if I can. And I hope that when people have seen Lady Landor received by you and, hope-fully, others, they will come to see her for what she is—a sweet and very gentle lady."

"You mean that she does not know that her own sister-in-law would do anything to ruin her socially?" Hugh demanded.

"She knows that Lady Ellis disliked her marrying her brother," Louisa said quietly. "But she knows nothing about the scandal Lady Ellis has been spreading. She thinks that all will go well be-tween them when they meet again. In fact, it was her notion to go to Lady Ellis this morning, until I dissuaded her by saying that it would be better to let her sister-in-law set the time and place. I said that, no doubt, she wanted to find a way to make it up between them."

"Then you have gone extremely far out on a limb, Miss Rogers," Lord Cardross observed, and she saw that his dark eyes were speculative. "Unless Lady Ellis can be convinced to change her mind, which I do not think very likely, Lady Landor is bound to find out the truth sooner or later."

"You do not give Miss Rogers credit for her ingenuity," the Duchess of Taxton said, putting in an appearance. "Hello, my dear. Miles. How nice to see you so soon again. And Claire. I missed you last night at Almack's. That is to say, I often saw you and Mr. Trever take the floor, but I never set eyes on you other-wise. You are a handsome couple. So handsome that I mean to send you off to talk to those two ladies over there. Now, my dear Miss Rogers. How did you fare with Lady Ellis? I hear that you were at her house this morning."

Louisa stared at the little birdlike woman in amazement. "But how on earth did you know that, madam?" she demanded. "Were you passing by in your carriage? Did you see me?"

She saw the duchess and Lord Cardross exchange amused glances. "Word travels very quickly among the *haut ton*," the duchess told her. "Which is only natural, I suppose, this being such a closed society. Oh, I am sorry, child. I did not mean to put it that way."

Louisa knew that her expression must have given her away. It was only that when the duchess had spoken of a closed society, she had realized, suddenly, what it would be like to be permanently outside it. Not because it offered much in the way of true brilliance. Not because anything about it could not be done without. But because, in the case of Lady Landor, there was no place else for her. Willy-nilly, she had a handle on her name. She must be with people like herself, and yet if Lady Ellis had her way, the door would be closed to her forever.

"The fact is," the duchess said confidentially, "that while I was at a whist party this afternoon, I heard a gentleman mention that Lady Ellis had spoken of having seen you. Indeed, he went on to elaborate about what he referred to as the 'difficulty' your father had created when he had left you in 'that woman's' care."

"Was it Sir Thomas Tigger?" Louisa demanded, clenching her hands.

"You know him, child?" the duchess said with a worried look.

"No," Louisa told her. "But I intend to make his acquaintance straight away."

Chapter Seven

"I expect that people are letting us get settled," Lady Landor said wistfully as she and Louisa sat in the sunny breakfast room two mornings later. "Of course, we have been invited to a soiree at the Duchess's on Thursday, but I had rather thought that we would be deluged with invitations by now."

She paused for a moment, looking at the bread and jam on her plate pensively. "I mean to say," she went on, "when we made an appearance at Almack's, we were saying that we were ready to appear socially."

Louisa did not know what to say. She had hoped that the patronage of Lady Cardross would be sufficient to reassure a few people, at least, of the propriety of making Lady Landor's acquaintance. It struck her now as quite significant that the party at Lady Cardross's had been small and private with no one except Hugh—who, after all, was almost part of the family—and the duchess to represent the world outside. Could it be that Lady Cardross had sent out other invitations which had been refused? The duchess had assured her on their first meeting that the Cardross name meant at great deal in the world of the *haut ton*. But, if what Louisa suspected was true, the lies that had been sent out about Lady Landor must have been too condemning to be overcome by the acceptance of one family, no matter how powerful that family might be.

"And I cannot understand why Lady Ellis has not made us a call or communicated in some way or other," Lady Landor continued, pushing her plate aside. She was, Louisa thought, beginning to show the effects of strain. The creamy skin was clearly affected by sleepless nights and even the chestnut hair did not seem so thick and lush. What a dreadful thing it would be if she should lanquish, Louisa thought. What a sad disappointment it would be for her father to return to London to find his bride-to-be a shadow of her former self and an exile from society, as well.

If nothing changed, Louisa told herself as she sipped her tea, she would have to tell Lady Landor the truth. What the effect of that would be, she did not know. No doubt she would rush off to Lady Ellis to ask her to withdraw her charges, and Louisa knew from personal experience how successful she was likely to be. And yet, how could she keep her from the woman? It was at precisely that moment that Louisa decided she would make good her promise to see Sir Thomas Tigger.

But how to go about it? To go to Lady Ellis and ask her to arrange a meeting was too much like admitting that she had some reason to think that his malice might be true. The duchess might have been at the same whist party with the gentleman, but Louisa thought that, from the way she had spoken of him, he was no more than someone whom she recognized and not a real acquaintance. She could not send a message to a total stranger, asking to see him. It would not do for her to seem unconventional, particularly under these circumstances when any out-of-the-way thing she might do would be ascribed to the unfortunate influence of Lady Landor.

As she tried to reassure her companion, one part of Louisa's mind continued to fret, but it was only after Lady Landor had declared that she had a migrim and would go and lie down, that Louisa made her decision. She would apply to Lord Cardross and see if he would help her.

Her message to him was answered instantly and, within the hour, it had been arranged that he would bring Sir Thomas to her that afternoon. "I do not know the gentleman except in passing," he wrote. "But I will approach him frankly and I do not think that he will refuse to see you. Further, I will see that my mother asks Lady Landor to ride out with her so that she will not be about when he and I make our call. I hope these efforts will help resolve the problem. Until then I remain yours faithfully, Miles Cardross."

At once Louisa felt her spirits lift. Surely he would not have agreed to arrange the meeting if he did not think that she might accomplish something. Unless, of course, he simply thought she ought to hear what Sir Thomas had to say. The idea made Louisa shiver, and she quickly tucked it away.

No, she would think of this afternoon as an occasion to make the gentleman understand the damage he was doing. If Lady Ellis was clearly without an eyewitness source for her stories, she would not even try to discover why he should have aired this slander in the first place. Doubtless he had some grudge or other, or perhaps he had simply confused Lady Landor with some other English lady.

The invitation for Lady Landor to ride out with Lady Cardross was brought by Claire herself with Hugh in attendance. "I am so sorry she has a migrim," she told Louisa as they sat together in the blue salon on a sunny windowseat, making a pretty picture, Louisa in her white, sprigged muslin gown, with the curls which escaped her mobcap framing her face, while Claire's fair charm was enhanced by her poke bonnet, which was decorated with pale blue taffeta to match her gown. As for Hugh, he stood watching them with smiling eyes. How fortunate they were, Louisa thought. They loved one another, and they had no cares. A sudden sense of loneliness overcame her even though that was absurd. Or so she told herself.

"Did you mother mean to have a party last night," she asked the girl on impulse. "I mean to say, did she invite a number of people and did they refuse when they knew that Lady Landor and I would be there?"

"Why, whatever made you think of such nonsense!" the girl declared, taking Louisa's hand in hers. "I assure you that no one refuses mama's invitations. Why, she might invite a Lucretia Borgia . . ."

She broke off, flushing. "But, of course, that is not what I mean," she said.

It was too late, of course. Whether she knew it or not, even Claire had her doubts. Perhaps she had heard some of the stories Lady Ellis was circulating, with the assistance of Sir Thomas Tigger. Louisa realized that one of the things she must know was what those stories were. It would not be enough, that afternoon, to beg Sir Thomas to keep silent, to refute what he had already said. It would not be enough to attempt to prove that he was wrong or that he had confused Lady Landor with some other person. She must know the full extent of the damage which had already been done.

"Mama only asked the people who attended," Claire was saying. "You and Lady Landor, the Duchess and Hugh. She thought that would make a pleasant beginning to our friendship, rather than a large affair where we probably would not have seen one another the entire evening. What a pity that you should have thought anything otherwise.''

''The duchess is the person who means to give you your real introduction to society,'' Hugh volunteered. What a youthful air he had about him, Louisa thought. The sort of air that she doubted would ever go away, as long as his fair hair could be worn tousled so becomingly and his outlook remained so boyishly direct. ''She has invited over fifty people.''

''Skimming the cream off the top, she calls it,'' Claire said with a laugh. ''There is to be an orchestra and we will dance all evening long.''

''Will it be known that Lady Landor and I will be attending?'' Louisa said in a low voice, keeping her thick-fringed eyes on Claire's pretty face, to watch for any play of feature which might contradict what was being said.

But the girl's expression was as open as Hugh's. ''They have been invited expecially to meet you both,'' she said quite cheerfully. ''The duchess says there is to be a reception line. And everyone has accepted. So you are not to worry! Promise me.''

It came to Louisa that perhaps people were coming out of curiosity. Simply agreeing to meet Lady Landor carried with it no responsibility of a social nature. They need not accept her. Make her their friend. And then she told herself that she was carrying suspicion too far. These people had been chosen by the duchess. Presumably they were her special friends, and not the sort of people who would have the motive she had silently attributed to them.

Relieved, Louisa let herself relax, and she and Claire were laughing at something Hugh had said when the door opened and Lady Landor came into the room, still in dishabille but with her color much restored. Indeed, her brocade and silk dressing gown, brilliant with peacock shades, made her lush beauty more apparent than Louisa thought she ever had seen it before. Apparently she had just risen from her rest, and her luxuriant chestnut hair was streaming down about her shoulders and her eyes were still heavy-lidded with her sleep.

''So we have visitors!'' she cried, clearly delighted. ''You should have let me know, Louisa. Claire, my dear. How good it is to see you. And Mr. Trever!''

It was only natural, Louisa supposed, that she should take the young man's hand. After all, she had taken Claire's in greeting. And as for the way she had looked at him, that was her ordinary expression. It was only her imagination that she thought she saw Claire's eyes narrow for a second.

"You cannot think how pleased I am to receive company," Lady Landor continued, settling herself on the settee and patting the red and silver striped satin of the cushion next to her in such a way that it was only natural that Hugh should take his place beside her. "In Florence there were always people about, and although I could not understand them, I became accustomed to being in a company. You understand, I know."

So saying, she looked first at Claire and then at the young man by her side with such an imploring manner that they could not help but respond.

"You were in Florence for a long time?" the girl asked her with a smile that was only a little forced.

"All the fifteen years of my marriage," Lady Landor replied with a small shrug of her lovely shoulders, as though those had been lost years indeed—as Louisa had no doubt they had been.

"And yet you did not learn to speak Italian?" Claire replied. "How very strange."

Louisa was certain that there was nothing spiteful about the girl. And yet there was a certain sting in what she had just said. She wondered if perhaps it might be that Lady Landor, behaving in quite a natural way, was seen to be a flirt by others, even when she did not mean a thing by what she did. Arranging for Hugh to sit beside her, for example. And just by being beautiful, which she could not help. Louisa noticed that the young man was staring at her almost as though he had been hypnotized. Claire could not help but notice that.

"I suppose it was," Lady Landor told her. "I sometimes think now that it was because I did not want to be there. It was a very lonely time for me and not to speak the language was my rebellion, perhaps. At least that was what Alfred used to say, and he was considered most perceptive by all his friends."

There was pathos about her, and Louisa did not doubt that it was real. But somehow she wished that Lady Landor had chosen some other subject, even though it was natural enough that she should speak of Florence.

"And did you have no English friends, madam?" Claire asked her, making Louisa wonder if she was making polite conversation or conducting an inquiry for reasons of her own. And then she hated herself for doubting the fair-haired beauty beside her. Why was it that she was seeing everything with doubled-visioned eyes? People were not like playing cards, one thing on one side, another if reversed.

"English friends," Lady Landor said vaguely. "Oh, there was a small community of English people. But my husband avoided them. He said they reminded him of everything that he had left behind. 'That dingy little island,' he used to say. Oh, dear, he hated the weather and the people, I do not know in what order. And he thought Florence was an Eden with its sunlight and the architecture and the art. But there! It makes me sad to remember. I only want to look into the future. You understand."

This time she only looked at Hugh, and that young man was apparently so struck by her past plight that, involuntarily, he put out his hand and covered her fingers with it on the red and silver satin cushion. Louisa saw the anger flash in the eyes of the girl beside her and thought it best to intervene.

"Claire has come with a message from her mother," she told Lady Landor. "You are to ride with her this afternoon if you will."

"I mean to accompany my mother," Claire said with a smile. "At least, I think I do. Certainly I will do so if you mean to help make up the party, Louisa."

"It must have been quite dreadful for you," both girls heard Hugh say. "Without friends and in a strange country."

"I am afraid that I have been guilty of self-pity," Lady Landor said with a little laugh. "It is a fault I try not to be guilty of. I have a great deal to be grateful for, and it is only vanity which makes me sad over my lost youth . . . But there! This will not do. It will not do at all."

And she dabbed at her eyes quite delicately enough to mask whether there were or were not any tears to remove. Suddenly Louisa found herself wondering if her father had heard the same words on the Bay of Biscay during that fateful voyage. Had he, perhaps, helped her to dry her tears? Had he looked at her as Hugh was looking now.

"Why, madam, you must not speak of having lost your youth," he exclaimed in a boyish way. "Damme if you are not the most beautiful . . ."

Louisa saw the necessity of stopping him before he had gone too far and wondered when he would have sense enough to notice the sheer rage on Claire's usually smiling face. But then he could not see her expression when he kept his eyes so exclusively on Lady Landor.

"I only hope that I can be a quarter as beautiful when I am your age," Louisa told the older woman, cutting Hugh off in mid-phrase. "And you are right. Why should you look backward when the future offers so much."

"That is precisely what your dear father says," Lady Landor declared, shifting her full attention to Louisa. A moment ago the girl could have sworn that Lady Landor was deliberately flirting with the young man beside her, but now she quite appeared to have forgotten him as she went on about the captain in a most complimentary way. Perhaps, Louisa told herself, she simply acts the way she does out of habit. Perhaps it is only her way. Certainly, in the case of Hugh she could have meant nothing by it. After all, he was half her age and engaged to Claire.

To smooth over the awkward moment or two which followed, Louisa explained that she would not ride out this afternoon, not giving any reason as Miss Patterson had often told her to do. "A lady who is confident never apologizes or explains," the headmistress had told her. And, although Louisa thought privately the maxim went too far, she chose to follow it in this instance and was relieved to see that no one asked her why.

On taking her departure, Claire seemed more puzzled than anything, for, although Hugh followed Lady Landor with his eyes, appearing to have been quite smitten, Her Ladyship was busy discussing what she intended to wear on her little outing, having apparently forgotten he was in the room.

"She is like that with everyone," Louisa whispered as she and Claire were about to leave. "She does not mean a bit of harm, you know. She is simply a very frank and open person."

"Yes," Claire said absently. "I hope that is the case, Louisa."

And, following her gaze, Louisa saw that Claire was looking at the letter from her brother which was on the table by the door. Had she, Louisa wondered, recognized the writing? Because if she had, it could mean that not only Lady Landor but Louisa herself might be suspect in Claire's eyes.

But there was no time to think on the matter for a knock came at the door and, to Louisa's considerable surprise, Michelle Rioux and her brother were being ushered into the hall.

Chapter Eight

"**I** confess I understand your point of view, Miss Rogers," Sir Thomas said, sipping his cup of tea with his little finger stuck out politely. "You have my sympathies completely. But I am obliged to report what I have seen with my own two eyes, you know. It would not do to lie or otherwise prevaricate. I would soon lose my credibility."

Louisa nodded and tried to keep her mind on what the gentleman was saying. Somehow it had been unduly upsetting for Michelle and her brother to arrive the way they had just as Claire and Hugh and Lady Landor were leaving. It had been necessary to perform introductions, of course, and Lady Landor, frank as usual, had expressed her surprise that Louisa could have come to know their neighbors and not once mention Mademoiselle and Monsieur Rioux to her.

Claire and Hugh, on the other hand, had seemed to see nothing at all curious in it, particularly when Louisa explained the meeting in the park. Indeed, they had been very good natured to the two strangers, conversing with them in French with a rapidity Louisa envied, and assuring them they would be eager to meet again. It had been impossible, of course, for them to linger, Lady Cardross waiting for them as she was. But the leave-taking had been genial and Michelle had smiled her pleasure when the door was closed behind them. Even her brother had seemed less dour than usual.

"Voilà," Michelle had exclaimed. "There are two well met and others yet to follow. We saw them from the window, *mon amie*, when they arrived. I hope you do not mind that we took advantage of the opportunity, one which was, no doubt, unexpected."

Having said which, she had looked at Louisa with such trusting eyes that the girl had known she must advise her and her brother that Sir Thomas Tigger and Lord Cardross also were to be visitors this afternoon.

"But I must speak to them privately," she added. "It is a personal matter . . ."

"Do not tell us anything, I beg you," Michelle had cried. "And you will have your private conversation. But we will stay just long enough to bid the gentlemen bonjour, if you do not mind."

They had made good Michelle's promise. When Lord Cardross and Sir Thomas had arrived a few moments later, they had allowed themselves to be introduced as visitors who were just leaving. Then they had been on their way, their purpose accomplished. And Louisa had been too distracted to notice whether Claude had examined these gentlemen as penetratingly as he had Claire and her brother. Indeed, she had been aware of some resentment since her first ambition was to greet Sir Thomas as calmly and coolly as possible. As it was, the intervention of her French neighbors had slightly put her off the mark. Given those circumstances, she felt now that she had not done too badly. Particularly now when he was making such a moderate reply.

Actually Sir Thomas was a very ordinary person of average height and looks, but he chose to deck himself out with such distinction that he must of needs be classified as a fop of the first water. His breeches were of the finest yellow nankeen imported from China, and his waistcoat was quilted, as Beau Brummel dictated. His white collar was starched, and he wore two cravats, black satin over white lawn. What little hair he had was fluffed and primped around his face in what Louisa thought was called the Brutus fashion. As to his manner, it was arch, and he carried himself in such a way as to make the effect that all his movements were on tiptoe, even though they clearly were not.

"Surely, Sir Thomas," Louisa said with great deliberation, "you do not expect me to believe that Lady Landor is the sort of person you have portrayed."

"What? Have you heard the stories? I am sorry for it, my dear." His very ordinary eyes bulged slightly out of sympathy. "I see that you are fond of Lady Landor. Or perhaps you only try to be in order to make your father happy."

"I am fond of her," Louisa said. "And I am certain of her character. As to your stories, I have not heard a one of them directly.

But I know their gist, and that is quite sufficient for me. Tell me, sir, when were you last in Florence?''

Louisa saw the faint smile which hovered about the gentleman's lips and guessed that he was complying with her request with some amusement. Clearly people interested him above all else. Perhaps this encounter would make a story for him to dine out on.

''Why, you should have heard the way the chit interrogated me,'' she could heard him say. ''As though she were a magistrate. I do not envy Captain Rogers with a bold jade for a daughter and Lady Landor as his wife.''

The notion made Louisa's cheeks flush. She felt them burn and hated it. Lord Cardross would think that she was suffering from embarrassment, and such was not the case at all.

''I only ask,'' she went on, keeping her voice low and even, ''because I think you may have mistaken her for someone else.''

''Oh, dear me, no,'' Sir Thomas exclaimed with a laugh. ''I would know Lady Landor anywhere, I assure you. That chestnut hair alone will distinguish her wherever she goes.''

''But she told me that she did not mingle with the English community in Florence,'' Louisa protested. ''The Duke, her husband, did not care to mix with them.''

''That is true enough, Miss Rogers,'' Sir Thomas replied. ''The Duke *never* mixed.''

The implication was clear enough. Suddenly Louisa remembered that disconcerting moment when Lady Landor had confessed that she had lightened her sad moments by taking drastic measures. Could that mean that she had made her own friends? English friends? Friends about whom her husband knew nothing? Was this supposed to be the source of Sir Thomas's stories? Were they, perhaps, even worse than she had imagined them to be?

Louisa glanced at Lord Cardross and saw that he was watching her with a curious expression in his dark eyes. Did he think that she was getting into deeper water than she knew? Was he amused, as Sir Thomas clearly was, by her naïveté? Should she have tried harder to appear older than she was? What a child she must look with her mobcap and her curls and her pink muslin gown! Still, she did not care what anyone thought. She intended to persist.

''You did not answer my first question, I think, sir,'' she said to Sir Thomas. ''When were you last in Florence?''

Sir Thomas was a fastidious gentleman. You saw it in the neat way he deposited his cup and saucer on the table and the way he crossed his legs. "Why, I was there for a good part of the winter," he declared. "I often go there and to Rome in January and February."

And he smiled at Louisa in a self-satisfied sort of way which made her dislike him even more than she had before. There was nothing at all exceptional about him except the foppishness of his dress, and yet he managed to make her feel that he did nothing but condescend. He had condescended to come here, he had condescended to answer her questions . . . Louisa hoped that she could keep her temper long enough to conduct this interview as she meant to—coolly, and with dispassion.

"And did you see Lady Landor on your last visit, sir?" she asked him. "Her husband, the Duke, had died the summer before, you will recall."

The trap she had set for him was about to close, and Louisa only wished that she had been able to tell Lord Cardross about it so that, when the moment came, he could see Sir Thomas as the villain he was. It would not be the same when she told him later that the months they were discussing were months when Lady Landor had remained in Florence only because the death of her husband had left her tired and ill. If Sir Thomas dared to say that he *had* seen her about in society, then the case would be proved against him. Louisa could threaten then, warn him that here was something she could prove. And if he could be found out in one lie, then she could easily discredit him. Louisa was not accustomed to being unscrupulous, but given what seemed to be Sir Thomas's character, that seemed to be her only hope. How arrogant he must be to have said the things he had about Lady Landor and yet, this very moment, be sitting in her drawing room, with no mention of apology to the daughter of the man she was to marry.

"Did I see Lady Landor this winter?" Sir Thomas mused. "But of course I did, Miss Rogers. It would have been a strange thing if I had not."

Louisa moved to the edge of her chair, hoping that her excitement would not show. Sir Thomas was about to fall into the trap.

"And could you be more particular, sir?" she asked him. "Where did you see the lady? Under what circumstances?"

Sir Thomas narrowed his eyes in a very ordinary sort of way. "Perhaps you can tell me first why you want to know, Miss Rogers," he said.

Louisa was ready for him. She had guessed this question would be asked. Doubtless the gentleman had come here determined to face up to her accusations that he had been unfair. Perhaps the fact that she had showed no emotion, made no demands, had set him off his guard.

"Lady Ellis said that I should talk to you," the girl replied, fixing him with one of the most intense looks she could manage in order to seem perfectly sincere. "She said that when I had heard what you had to tell me about Lady Landor, I would see that it was quite out of the question for me to live here, let alone allow my father to marry her. That is why I want to know particulars."

She knew that Lord Cardross was looking at her curiously and she wished that she had told him, in her letter, precisely what she had in mind. Was he thinking now, she wondered, that she was actually ready to believe the slander about Lady Landor? Did he think that she would go behind her patroness's back in such a way? Yes, she was afraid he did. There was something about the look on his dark face. . . . And then he moved a bit away from them, a handsome figure in his blue jacket and buckskin breeches with highly polished Hessian boots. Silently she begged him not to go beyond earshot, for it was vital to her that he overhear everything Sir Thomas had to say.

"It was Lady Ellis's impression that you did not intend to talk to me, Miss Rogers," Sir Thomas said, examining his watch chain to see that the two watches which hung from it, one on either side of his waistcoat, were situated in a uniform way.

"That was my first reaction," Louisa told him. "Of course I was dismayed. But later I had time to think quite seriously about the matter, and I realized that it was simply not conceivable that you should make up outright lies. Unless, of course, you had some reason to want to malign the lady."

Sir Thomas raised his very ordinary eyebrows and assumed a look of mild disdain. "I have no wish to malign anyone, Miss Rogers," he assured her.

"You only think that the truth should be told about everyone," Louisa pressed him. "As far, that is, as it can be ascertained."

"Yes, that is it exactly," he assured her.

"And would you say that more time is spent in collecting slander than in finding that in men and women to commend?" Louisa continued, knowing that she was off the track, knowing that she was close to losing her temper, but unable to restrain.

Sir Thomas smiled down his nose at her. "I do not *collect* news, Miss Rogers. That can be left to the newsgrubbers on Fleet Street, I hope. But as to what I hear and see, I fear it is apt to be unpleasant more than the contrary, human nature being what it is. I have often found that most unfortunate. Human folly, I mean. There is so very much of it."

"Yes," Louisa told him. "Certainly there does not seem to be a need for invention as to folly. Unless, of course, someone like Lady Ellis might like to blacken someone else's name. Would she come to you, do you think, Sir Thomas, for particular information?"

"You are a curious young lady, Miss Rogers," Sir Thomas said, making a steeple of his fingers to prop his chin on. "You ask me to come here, presumably to find out what I know about Lady Landor. You ask, in fact, for particulars. And then you proceed to insult me by saying straight out that I supply information to order. You must learn to be more subtle, do you not agree, Lord Cardross?"

The young viscount had been standing by the window, but now he turned to face them. "I think her point is clear enough," he said. "Subtlety would do little to improve it."

"Well, then, I will bow to your opinion, sir," Sir Thomas said, looking at Louisa with mocking eyes. "You ask me if I supply Lady Ellis with information. Why, so I have done over the years. She is my friend. We talk, as friends are wont to do. I spent time in Florence, which is where her brother lives . . . or, rather, lived. Lady Ellis was very bitter when she heard of his death, you know, and, I thought, with good reason. He was buried there, you know. In Florence. That was his widow's doing. His family did not even know of his passing until he was underground."

"You have a direct way of putting things," Louisa observed dryly. "You make it appear that Lady Landor was guilty of something in the way you tell that story, and I expect in every other that you repeat about her. The fact is that in a climate such as that of Florence it is quite usual, I believe, for burials to take place immediately. There would have been no time for the family to be summoned, even if the Duke had wanted it, which the evidence denies."

"What evidence, my dear Miss Rogers?"

"He tore up his sister's letters without reading them. He never returned to England. He wanted nothing more to do with Lady Ellis after the way she behaved on hearing how he meant to marry."

Sir Thomas smiled complacently. "A pretty story," he told her. "You tell it very well. Is that what Lady Landor has led you to believe."

"It is the truth," Louisa told him. "How can you doubt it?"

"*Someone* may have torn up the Duke's letters from his sister," Sir Thomas declared. "*Someone* may have made certain that they never returned to England. But not necessarily the Duke, Miss Rogers. Not necessarily the Duke."

Louisa could feel her self-possession fading. "The Duke had a passion for Florence," she exclaimed. "That was common knowledge, sir."

"Oh, have you spoken to many people who knew him? Have you, perhaps, friends in Florence who can verify that he stayed there of his own accord and not because the wife on whom he doted had convinced him that, without the gentle climate, she would fade away and die?"

He was too persuasive for Louisa to allow him to go on. The girl was aware of the quick way in which Lord Cardross had turned his attention to him, and knew that he was giving what the man said serious consideration. But she could not, *would* not believe him. What a picture he painted. A wife who manipulated her husband to keep him abroad. A woman who, far from being isolated by her husband's friends whose tongue she did not speak, had much to do with the English-speaking community in the city. He wanted her to believe that Lady Landor actually caused the breach between her husband and his sister by tearing up the letters he received. Were these the stories he had been telling? Was this the monster he had created? No wonder there had been that great silence when they had first come to Almack's. No wonder no invitations had been received. It was a wonder that Lady Cardross had received them, even if her son was a close friend of Louisa's father.

Sir Thomas was right. How could she prove that what he said was false? She knew no one in Florence. Even if someone—perhaps Lady Cardross—knew someone there to whom she might write, it would take too long. The damage would be done. *Had* been done. Even her trick . . . How naïve she had been to think that it might work. But, all the same, she meant to try it.

"You said you saw Lady Landor this winter," Louisa said as evenly as she was able. "After her husband's death."

"Why, yes. I saw her often," Sir Thomas replied. "She was at a soiree given in honor of . . ."

"That is impossible, sir!" Louisa replied, rising to her feet in a whirl of embroidered muslin. "Lady Landor was ill after her husband's death. It was a long illness and kept her there in Florence for many months. She attended no soirees, sir. Even had she been well, she would not have done so, since she was in mourning."

Sir Thomas tapped his teeth with one finger and then he, too, rose and made a bow.

"You have accused me of deliberately lying, Miss Rogers," he said with a frown. "In the company of a witness. I could, if I wanted, take the matter to court. That would make an ideal public forum, would it not? We could be certain that the entire world would know the truth about the lady your father intends to marry. Have it printed up in broadsheets. Is that what you want, I wonder? Is that really what you want?"

"You may threaten me all you want," Louisa exclaimed, in a proper temper now. "But I know that you are wrong. Deliberately wrong. You mean to hurt her. Why?"

"And you dare to speak to me of slander, Miss Rogers," Sir Thomas said with a sneer. "You may hear from my soliciter. I can promise nothing."

With which announcement, he started for the door just as it opened and Lady Landor came into the room. She was smiling and her cheeks glowed from the fresh air.

But then she saw Sir Thomas, and she gasped a word which would not come. Her face went white and whiter still until every vestige of color had drained away. And then, before Lord Cardross could catch her, she crumpled to the floor in a deep swoon.

Chapter Nine

"IT was kind of you to wait, sir," Louisa told Lord Cardross an hour later when she joined him in the small garden at the back of the house. "Lady Landor is resting now, quite recovered from her faint."

Late afternoon sunlight was pouring down onto the roses, which nodded their heads in the shelter of the stone wall enclosing them, and the air was full of sweet smells that made Louisa remember the country and the walks she had taken as a schoolgirl. How far behind her that all seemed. Ugly marks had been left on recent memories, particularly today. She had not wanted to believe Sir Thomas. She did *not* believe him. But he had tarnished everything. Nothing could ever again be quite the same. He had made her appear to behave like the kind of person she did not want to be. She had leaped into the fray without doubting that she would succeed. Oh, it was all to have been simple! Both with Lady Ellis and Sir Thomas. What had ever made her think she could outwit them?

"Allow me to say that you appear to be distressed, Miss Rogers," Lord Cardross said. "Is there anything that I can say and do . . . ?"

"You can tell me that I am a fool," Louisa said with feeling. "I know I feel one."

"Because you lost your temper?" he asked her, strolling beside her as she paced the gravel path striking one hand against the other. "I will admit you flare up quickly."

He was smiling. She amused him. Oh, this was worse than she had feared! The sheer humiliation of it was more than she could bear. She was still so far from composure that she had not even bothered to tidy her tangled curls when she had left Lady Landor, revived, to Maria's silent care.

"I will not keep you longer, sir," she told him stiffly. "Thank you for bringing Sir—Sir Thomas here. After what you have heard, you may not want to keep our company again. I mean by that, you have my permission to tell your mother and your sister and the duchess. . . . I mean, I will quite understand if you want to warn them that they may have been quite wrong about Lady Landor. That my father may have been mistaken in his estimate of her character.''

His dark eyes seemed to burn hers as he took her arm and brought her, almost precipitously, to a halt.

''Do you mean that you no longer believe her to be innocent of the charges which have been made against her?'' he demanded.

''No! She is innocent. I am certain of it.'' Louisa replied. ''My father would not have offered for her otherwise.''

''Your father is my friend, and I respect him,'' the young viscount said in a low voice. ''But he is only human. All of us can make mistakes, fall in love with the wrong people, see them in a different light.''

''By that you mean that you believe Sir Thomas,'' Louisa said with a toss of her dark curls. The thickly fringed green eyes were blazing as she pulled herself away from him.

''You are too quick to jump to conclusions,'' Lord Cardross told her. ''There is room for doubt. That much seems clear. And, at the moment, we only have her word against his. As for my mother and the other, I see no need to repeat what Sir Thomas said. No doubt they have heard some of it already and will hear the rest before they are done.''

''Along with everyone else in London,'' Louisa murmured. ''Oh, I *do* feel such a fool. I meant to put a stop to all the rumors, and instead I seem to have made everything worse.'' Her laughter had a bitter tinge. ''Only think! He threatened to sue me for slander.''

''He meant nothing by it,'' Lord Cardross assured her. ''He is the sort of chap to respond to an attack with one. That is not what troubles me.''

There was a stone bench in the corner where most of the sun was trapped, and Louisa sat down on it. Strange that on such a warm day she should feel a chill. It was good of Lord Cardross not to tell her that she had been a fool. He was very patient with her. No doubt he felt some responsibility as her father's friend.

Strangely enough, it was her father whom he mentioned next. ''While you and Sir Thomas were having at one another,'' he said dryly, ''something came to mind which I had not thought of before. And that is what will happen when your father returns to London.''

"I never thought that I would ever want him to stay away as long as possible,'' Louisa murmured. "But I find I do. Everything must be settled before he comes back. She must be established in society and . . . But what occurred to you?''

Lord Cardross looked down at her thoughtfully. His dark eyes and handsome face seemed as familiar to her as though she had known him for years.

"I do not want to upset you, Miss Rogers,'' he said with a formality she hated, "but if matters are not settled when he returns, I think it might be wise not to tell him the source of the rumors about Lady Landor which Lady Ellis is spreading.''

"But why?'' Louisa demanded. "He has a right to know.''

"And what do you think his response will be when he knows about Sir Thomas?'' he asked her, and again his tone was dry as though he wanted to remind her that she had thought nothing through at all. The implied rebuke pained her more than she was prepared to admit, even to herself.

"Why, he will be angry, of course. No doubt he will talk to Sir Thomas, as I have done.''

"I do not think the conversation would have been precisely the same this afternoon,'' Lord Cardross said, "had your father arranged it.''

"No doubt he would have been more forceful.''

"I think he would have been more than forceful, Miss Rogers. I think he would have called the fellow out.''

Louisa stared at him in horror. "A duel!'' she exclaimed. "You think he would have challenged him.''

"In a similar situation, that is what I would feel forced to do,'' he told her, and his eyes were very dark, even in the sunlight. "Any gentleman would, I think.''

He was right, of course. Louisa marveled that she had not thought of it herself. Here she had been, anticipating the pain with which her father would greet the situation if it remained unchanged. But she had come by her temper naturally. If she were angry, he would be enraged. The mere fact that duels were uncommon and frowned upon by law would make no difference. People fought them every day. Only last week she had heard of a young marquess who had been killed and his rival wounded.

Louisa became aware that she was clenching her hands so tightly that her fingernails were drawing blood. She pressed her open palms on the cool stone and looked up into Lord Cardross's face.

"Why, that is dreadful," she exclaimed. "It must be prevented at all costs. But how, if Sir Thomas is determined to ruin her? And since he thinks he has good reason . . ."

She bit her lip. She had not meant to say that. It would only make matters worse if anyone were to know what Lady Landor had told her not an hour since, as she had recovered her senses and lapsed into a fit of tears. Louisa realized that Lord Cardross must have guessed that some explaination of the swoon must have been made. It should have been the first question to be asked her when she had joined him in the garden. After all, Lady Landor had seemed quite well until she had set eyes on Sir Thomas. A certain inference was clear. And yet he had said nothing, only let her talk her way around to it. And now, having said so much, how could she refuse to tell him?

"Good reason?" he said in a low voice, his dark eyes never once leaving her face.

Louisa hesitated, trying to decide what was best.

"You do not have to tell me, of course," he went on. "I only want you to know that I am convinced it is a serious situation. Idle tattle can be forgotten. But Sir Thomas has made serious charges. And, if he has a reason to have resorted to malice . . ."

"She was too hysterical to tell me much," Louisa told him. "Maria went to fetch a vinagrette and while she was gone, Lady Landor told me that Sir Thomas had—had proposed himself to her. I can only guess at what she meant, for she was nearly incoherent. I thought at first that she meant that he had made her an offer long ago, when she was a girl. But she shook her head when I said as much. Her face was buried in her hands. And so it must have been when she was married. Sir Thomas must have pressed his attentions on her and been refused. And yet how could that be true when . . ."

"When she only met her husband's company?" Lord Cardross said. "When only Florentines were about her? When she was kept well away from the English circle in the city?"

There was no banter in his voice now, no irony. And Louisa guessed what he was thinking. That her father had been deceived. That it might well be that Lady Landor was all that Lady Ellis called her and worse. Suddenly there was so much evidence to support that! Seen in that light there was nothing innocent or charming about Lady Landor's ways. Her rides along The Mall became no mere amusements. The way she had elicited Hugh's sympathies this morning could give cause for alarm. The damage to Louisa's own reputation . . .

"That doesn't matter," she said aloud, rising from the stone bench.

Lord Cardross frowned. "What doesn't matter?" he demanded. "The fact that she may have been lying to your father and to you? The fact that . . . ."

"It was just something that I was thinking," Louisa told him. "Your points are well made. I mean to ask her how she came to meet Sir Thomas. She will want an explanation of why she found him with me, at all events."

"And do you mean to be open with her?"

Louisa spread her hands. "What choice do I have now?" she demanded. "I have made matters worse instead of better, haven't I? You should have stopped me."

For a moment he proceeded her as they walked along the gravel path. "I had no right to interfere," he said. "You are an extraordinary young lady, Miss Rogers. It is impossible to guess what you will do next."

"You think I am impulsive?"

"Perhaps." He slowed his pace to let her join him. "I would offer you advice if I thought that you would take it."

Louisa flushed. What a child he clearly thought her. And yet she must depend on someone. Wherever she stirred the waters, she only seemed to muddy them.

"Very well," she said. "What is it you think that I should do?"

They had moved out of the sun now, but the air was warm and rich with the scent of flowers. There was a breeze and, because Louisa had not thought to don a bonnet, it ran its fingers through her curls. Lord Cardross stood quite still and looked at her, a tall, handsome figure of a gentleman with shoulders so broad they strained the seams of the superfine of his blue jacket.

"I will try to find out what really happened in Florence," he told her. "Which means that I must try to find someone who was there, and has returned. Even if it were not for Napoleon, a letter would take too long. I think your father may be returning sooner than you think."

"You know a good deal about him and the secret work on which Wellington employs him, don't you?" Louisa said, struck by a sudden certainty that this was so. "Why, I would not be surprised to find that you know the exact day he will return."

"You have a lively imagination, Miss Rogers," Lord Cardross replied, and now the dry voice had returned. "Let us not change the subject, pray. If someone can be found—someone reliable—to tell us what really happened, what sort of woman Lady Landor was there, we will know what steps to take with some certainty of success."

"Unlike my vain endeavors?" Louisa said.

"It would be singularly foolish to pretend that you have had a great success with either Sir Thomas or Lady Ellis," he told her. "As I said before, you are impulsive. Your association with Mademoiselle and Monsieur Rioux is a case in point."

"But they are neighbors," Louisa protested.

For a moment he said nothing, and she could only hope she was not showing her discomfort. Perhaps he knew, better than she, what Michelle and her brother were about. After all, he knew something of her father's activities. Could it be possible that he knew what her French acquaintances were up to? Was he trying to warn her that she should have nothing to do with them? And, if so, why did he not speak directly to the point?

All these questions were in her mind, but, for some reason, all she said was that it was very kind of him to want to be of so much assistance. And if there was an edge of irony in her voice, well then she could not help it. At least that was what Louisa told herself when he was gone.

Chapter Ten

"WHATEVER happens, I want us to be friends," Claire told Louisa as, arm and arm, they made their way along the side of the busy street in the direction of the drapers where both girls meant to buy some cloth. "Wait! Have we lost poor Burtie? Mother always insists that one of the footmen go with me when I go on shopping expeditions. Unless she or Hugh are with me, of course."

"Lady Landor says the same," Louisa hastened to tell her. "No one could be more careful of the proprieties."

"As far as you are concerned, at any rate," Claire added, with a caustic note in her voice. "There is Burtie. Do you see? Just there. I will wave in his direction, for I believe he thinks that he has lost us in the crowd."

Bond Street, late on a spring morning, was indeed a busy place to be. The narrow, cobbled street was crowded with wagons, carts, and carriages, and it was necessary for pedestrians to look sharp as they made their way along past storefronts where diamond-paned windows bulged with goods for sale. When Louisa had received a note from Claire this morning, asking her to join in a shopping expedition, she had hoped that simply being out of the house and away in the thick of London would bring back some of the excitement she had first felt when she had come here.

And it was true enough that, in the bustle, her spirits rose. She had decked herself out for the occasion in a green taffeta pelisse with a high collar which made a pleasant contrast to her simple white, muslin gown, and she knew that her bonnet, with its flowered rim, was most becoming. Claire, too, looked her best in a blue cashmere shawl that matched the color of her morning gown, and they were attracting some attention—of the sort it would be natural for young girls to revel in. What a pity, Louisa thought, that when she saw someone look after her, all she could think was that they must know who she was. Still, she must accept the

71

fact that through Lady Landor she had been touched by the finger of notoriety and that it must leave a stain.

When she mentioned this to Claire, however, the girl laughed off the notion. "You are becoming too self-conscious," she told her. "After the Duchess's party, you will wonder why it was you ever worried."

And yet Louisa knew that Claire, for her own reasons, was no more certain of Lady Landor's character than she was. After all, there had been that morning when the older woman had aroused Hugh's sympathy in such a seemingly deliberate way. Louisa's own doubt had not crowded in on her until this morning when she finally had been admitted by a silent Maria into Lady Landor's bedchamber.

"What can you think of me?" the chestnut-haired beauty had demanded. "I cannot think what made me faint away like that. Perhaps it was because the sun was very warm when Lady Cardross and I went riding. After all, I only wore my Leghorn, and it *was* an open carriage."

Louisa had been afraid that she would make some excuse of that very sort, and her disappointment must have showed clear on her face, for Lady Landor had fidgeted with the blanket and made a great business of plumping pillows. All the while her eyes had asked some question of Louisa that, apparently, she could not put into words.

It had been the girl who had finally done it for her. "Yesterday," she said, "you indicated that some unpleasantness had passed between you and Sir Thomas in Florence."

Lady Landor was clearly flushed. "Yesterday," she said, "I was in such a state that I might have said anything. Anything at all!"

Louisa had known then that Lady Landor could be kept no longer in a fool's paradise as to what the true situation was.

"I had him come here," she said in a low voice, sinking down on the bottom of the bed, "because he is circulating stories about you. Unpleasant stories. And Lady Ellis repeats everything he says. That is the reason behind the lack of invitations. That is the reason we were greeted at Almack's as we were the other evening."

Nothing could really mar Lady Landor's lush beauty, but she did look pale and strained. Sinking back against the ruffled pillows, she rubbed the fine lawn of her dressing gown between thumb and finger, nervously.

"I guessed at something of the sort," she said at last. "It has never been any secret that my sister-in-law hates me. But I never thought that she would go this far. And as for Sir Thomas . . ."

"Did you know him?" Louisa demanded, leaning forward to put her hand on the older woman's arm, feeling the contrast between them more clearly than ever she had before—this beauty whom her father meant to marry, still in bed at ten in the morning while she was neatly outfitted for the day. And yet she brushed the thought away. Their habits might not be compatible, but she was fond of Lady Landor, and she meant to help her and, in so doing, to help herself.

"You must tell me the truth," Louisa told her, suddenly suffocated by the scented atmosphere of the richly decorated room. "Is there any truth in the stories Sir Thomas has been circulating?"
Lady Landor took up a handmirror which lay beside her in a welter of quilts and blankets, and examined her face. But it was clear that, although she pretended disinterest in the conversation, she was very much involved. Her clear need to buy time troubled Louisa.

"How can I tell," Lady Landor said with a shrug, "when I do not even know what he is saying? He was known in Florence as a scandalmonger of the worse sort."

"But I thought you kept yourself restricted to your husband's circle," Louisa had protested. "Italian people who had nothing to do with the English in Florence."

"And so I did," Lady Landor replied. "For the most part, that is. But sometimes—I told you the other day about my 'sad' dress—I would feel the need for company. I made friends with some English women. Rode with them of an afternoon. There is a lovely drive to the east on the hills above the city. And I was fond of the Boboli gardens. Alfred was not interested in expeditions except to see some ruin or other."

"Were those drives your—drastic measures?" Louisa asked her.

The words produced a dramatic explosion of the sort the girl had not expected. Tossing back the covers and sending the hand glass smashing to the floor, Lady Landor walked across the room, her nightgown streaming after her. When she whirled to face the girl, it was clear that she was angry.

"What right have you to question me this way?" she demanded. "Have you some sort of blackmail in mind? Unless I tell you everything you want to know, you will make a bad report to your father when he returns? Is that the answer? And what have you been up to behind my back? When you first learned that stories were being spread about me, why did you keep it a secret? And, if you believe them, what are you doing here? I have no wish to tarnish your reputation."

Louisa felt that most of what she said was deserved. The anger, although unexpected, was only natural. And yet it was clear at once that Lady Landor could not sustain it. She buried her lovely face in her hands, and her shoulders began to shake. Louise hurried to put her arm about her, press her down on the chaise longue at the foot of the bed, murmur conciliatory nothings.

"I must know everything," Lady Landor said at last, raising her tear-stained face and accepting the lacy handkerchief Louisa had at hand. "You understand that. You must!"

Louisa slipped to the floor beside her in a billow of white muslin. "I only heard by accident," she said, hoping to slip over that part. She had no wish to remember that afternoon with Mrs. Thrasher in the park. "And I did not tell you straight away because I did not want you to be sad. I thought that once we had made a few public excursions, people might see that you were someone they wanted to receive. But that was before I knew how bad the stories were. Oh dear! Are you sure you want to hear this?"

Lady Landor was reclining on the brocade-upholstered chaise with her eyes closed and one hand over them. "Tell me all," she murmured. "I must hear it all."

And so Louisa had told her, hating every word of it and watching Lady Landor's face. When she had finished, a great silence fell upon the room, a silence deep enough to make Louisa conscious of a creaking so slight that, in the ordinary way, she would not have heard it. Turning she saw the door closing slowly and realized that Maria must have elected to eavesdrop. What did it matter? She might as well know as not.

"So," Lady Landor said in a low voice. "I am a flirt, or worse. My husband stayed in Florence on my account. My contact with the English community there was much more intimate than I have ever said. I led my husband a merry chase. I was not ill after his death . . ."

"I did not say that I believe it," Louisa told her. "Certainly Lady Cardross and her family do not. And the guests at the Duchess's party are coming particularly to meet you."

Lady Landor's eyes had never seemed a richer brown. "And your father?" she asked the girl.

"How can you even imagine that he would listen to such stories?" Louisa demanded. "Indeed, it is Lord Cardross's opinion . . ."

"It is strange to think of all of you chatting away about me behind my back," the older woman said with the only tinge of bitterness Louisa had ever heard in her voice. "But, no matter. What *is* his opinion?"

"He—he thinks papa may very well challenge Sir Thomas to a duel when he discovers the malice he has spread," Louisa told her.

Lady Landor threw back her head and laughed. Indeed, she laughed so wildly that Louisa was afraid that she was falling into hysteria and wondered if Maria should be called. But, in a moment, the laughter stopped as abruptly as it had begun.

"So now, in addition to all the rest of it, I can anticipate the honor of being responsible for putting your father in danger of his life," she said. "As though the army were not enough, he can return to London and be privileged to discover that he is affianced to someone whose very name has become a scandal, that he has entrusted his daughter to her with the result that she is *personna non grata,* too, and that in order to maintain even a shred of honor, he must duel a gentleman who is not worthy to so much as shine his boots."

It had been the first time Louisa had ever heard bitterness like this from Lady Landor, and she found she hated it. She had so much wanted her to be the simple, cheerful person who followed impulse innocently enough. Yes, she must admit it. There had been charm in the notion that for fifteen years this exotic woman had been kept isolated from the world, with an adoring husband and a ring of friends who loved him and, consequently, her.

"You are not at fault," Louisa told her. "It would be absurd to blame yourself."

"I was at fault when I married as I did," Lady Landor told her vehemently. "I thought that if he was kind and generous, it would be enough. But then—the days were endless. Endless! And I was young and spirited. Surely it was only natural . . ."

She had paused and raised herself from her reclining position on the chaise, had taken Louisa's hand and pressed it. Now, standing in the musty draper's shop with Claire, examining one bolt of satin after another, Louisa remembered the sweet lemon odor of the older woman's scent.

"All I did was to take rides with Englishwomen," she had told her. "Made friends of them. And sometimes I took tea. That was how it happened that I met Sir Thomas. He importuned me from the start. I do not think he could believe that someone like myself, married to an older husband who was something of a recluse, could resist his advances."

"But you did resist?"

"More than that. I withdrew completely from English society until he had left Florence. But the gentleman is persistant. The next year when he came on his visit, he renewed the attack and drove me into isolation again. And so it went. At last—two years ago—I decided to stop retreating. Alfred did not mind the afternoons I spent away. He understood my need to talk to my own countrymen, even though he had no liking for them."

"Did you tell him about Sir Thomas?"

"Oh, no. He would have been disturbed. I never troubled him. Yes, I can say that in all fairness. It was my part of the bargain, you see. I never, ever troubled him."

But the feeling of relief with which Louisa had left Lady Landor after the explanation, lucid and as likely as it was, was not lasting. Now, while one of the thin clerks bustled about behind the counter, searching for a bolt of silk to match a piece Claire had brought with her, Louisa wondered why. It was not fair to her father. Certainly it was not fair to Lady Landor. Why did she find it so difficult to believe her? Was it a testimony to the virulence of Sir Thomas's slander?

"There now," Claire said. "I am almost finished. As soon as he has found the silk . . . But, only look! There is Lady Ellis. And her three daughters. They have not seen you yet. Do you intend to snub them?"

"No doubt they will take the first opportunity to snub me," Louisa replied, remembering that Claire might know nothing of her visit to Lady Ellis. Granted that the duchess had seen her leaving the house, but she had brought it up when only Lord Cardross was in attendance. It might be that everyone had kept quiet on the subject. For the first time, it occurred to her to wonder precisely how much Claire did know. She had seen the way she looked at the letter covered with her brother's writing the other morning. Clearly she did not know that she had been sent to offer Lady Landor a ride out with her mother specifically because Sir Thomas was being brought to the house.

"Lady Ellis is coming this way," Claire said in a whisper as the clerk presented the bolt of cloth. "Do you mean to keep your back turned? It would, at least, avoid an awkward situation."

But, before Louisa could make reply, or even, for that matter, make up her mind, she heard the familiar, rasping voice behind her, calling her by name.

"My dear Miss Rogers," Lady Ellis said. "And this *is* Miss Cardross, I believe. I think we were introduced to one another years ago. You both know my daughters, I think. What a lovely day it is! Far too nice to spend in shops, I think. Sir Thomas told me that he and you had a lovely conversation, Miss Rogers. I am so glad you took my word and listened to what he had to say."

She paused for breath, looking thin as a quill, as always, and with feathers bravely waving. Behind her in the shop's gloom, Patience cast her eyes in two directions, Fanny showed her teeth, and Horatia looked at the girls down her slanted nose.

"And then I have had occasion to speak to Mrs. Thrasher," Lady Ellis continued. "Did you know that your headmistress is to be in town? Yes, Miss Patterson, I believe. She will pretend that she came on her own business, but a little bird has told me that she is concerned about you. As well she should be, even though you are no longer her charge, Miss Rogers. Yes, I believe you will be hearing from her presently, and when you do, I hope you will take the better part of wisdom and listen to her advice."

Chapter Eleven

"Bᴜᴛ, of course, she is quite charming," Miss Patterson was telling Louisa the next morning just after Lady Landor had excused herself and left the room. "She knew that we would want to talk together privately, and she made it seem the natural thing. It would appear that she should bring your father good fortune."

"It *should* appear that she would," Louisa answered. "But you know more about the situation than to believe that it will be true."

Louisa's former headmistress was a quiet-looking woman with jet black hair which she pulled tight to the back of her head in a chignon. Of middle years, she still boasted skin without a wrinkle and made, Louisa often thought, an affectation of her gold-rimmed spectacles which she used so little that they spent most of the time on her snub nose.

During the ten years Louisa had spent at the academy, she had learned to love Miss Patterson as well as to respect her. As a lonely child, missing her mother, she had found the headmistress compassionate but not cloying. Never once did she pretend to Louisa that their relationship was anything other than it was, but neither did she make a secret of how fond she was of the little girl with the dark curls and thickly fringed blue eyes.

When it had become apparent that Louisa was very intelligent, Miss Patterson had exposed her to the sorts of studies not generally thought proper for young ladies. As a result, although Louisa made no boast of it, she could read and write both Greek and Latin as well as any young man down from Eton, and also was knowledgeable in mathematics and history. But it had been literature which had brought her her greatest pleasure, and these lessons she had received in private from the headmistress, who had not troubled to disguise her delight that her favorite shared her love of the classics. And so their relationship had grown and mellowed.

Valerie Bradstreet

Never once had Miss Patterson offered advice except when Louisa asked for it, and that seemed the pattern she meant to follow now.

"Since I had business in London," she told Louisa, peering at her over her gold-rimmed glasses, "I thought that I would get in touch with you."

"And are you staying with Mrs. Thrasher?" Louisa asked her.

"After your letter, I could scarcely do that," the headmistress said simply. "I advised her that I was arriving in the city and that I preferred to put up at an inn. She is a second cousin. We were never close. I was appalled by what you told me, and I hoped, somehow, that I might made amends."

"But you have nothing to make amends for," Louisa told her, taking her hands. "I would have heard what Mrs. Thrasher had to tell me from someone else. Indeed, it was as well that I was warned."

And, with that, she made a brief summary of everything that had happened, to all of which the other woman listened closely.

"What of you?" she said when Louisa had finished. "I seem to have heard a good deal of Lady Landor, who may or may not have been maligned. But I confess to being more concerned with your happiness, Louisa. In all of this, have you not forgotten yourself?"

The morning light sent thin shafts through the windows onto the pianoforte, and Louisa remembered that, had she been at the school, this would have been the time for her music practice. How strange it was that, since she had come to London, she had not touched the pianoforte. And as for thinking of her own happiness, surely that was wrapped up so closely with Lady Landor . . .

"You are a strong person, my dear Louisa," Miss Patterson was saying with the vehemence with which she always made her points. "All this nonsense about the tarnish of scandal . . ."

"You have been talking with Mrs. Thrasher."

"No," the headmistress said with a little moue. "But I received a letter from her, and that was a phrase she used. The point I want to make is that you are *you* and not the reflection of someone else. And as for being influenced, Mrs. Thrasher and the others may not know it but I am certain that you could have lived with Lady Macbeth and kept your full integrity. I am not drawing a comparison, mind you."

She had always been able to make Louisa laugh as she did now. It was a side of herself the older woman did not often show, cer-

80

tainly not to the teachers whom she employed. "Perhaps it gives me pleasure to see you laugh," she had once told the girl when her reading of a passage of Fielding's *Tom Jones* had sent Louisa into gales of laughter. Yes, Miss Patterson was a strange mixture of perfect decorum and the odd impropriety—such as the reading not only of Fielding's novels but Richardson's as well. And she and Louisa shared a passion for Restoration plays that, like *The School for Scandal*, showed a certain reckless disregard for the conventions.

"There now. That is better," the headmistress said with a little tick of her tongue to show her full approval. "Is it as long a time since you have laughed as I think?"

"Too long," Louisa told her. "But now we must be serious, and you must give me your impressions."

Miss Patterson stiffened her shoulders in the gray merino dress and assumed a prim, schoolmarm expression. Louisa fought the impulse to fall into another laugh.

"My impression, my dear," the older woman told her, "is that you are very nicely placed, in a charming house with a lady for company who has not only the recommendation of your father's deep regard but of her own beauty and a gentle, friendly nature. There have been no orgies held, I take it. You will remember the Roman revels described in your Suetonius. No celebrations on the level of those held by Tiberius when he lived at Naples. Ah, my dear, the advantages of a classical education! Such . . . pleasant reading, was it not? No one will take your place, you know. But, enough of pathos. You asked for my impressions, and I have given them."

Louisa had not been at all certain of what advice she would be given when she asked for it, but this took her by surprise. Miss Patterson had paid Lady Landor close attention and apparently had found nothing suspicious about her.

"Does that mean," she said now, "that you think I should put no stock in the rumors?"

"I think you can only trust the evidence of your own eyes," the headmistress told her. "Have you ever seen her play the flirt, for instance?"

Louisa remembered those few moments here in this same room when Lady Landor had evoked Hugh Trever's sympathies so artfully. She remembered hands touching and a certain smile.

"Perhaps once or twice," she ventured.

"And how long have you been living with her? More than a week, I warrant." Miss Patterson threw out both hands in one of the dramatic gestures she sometimes indulged in. "My dear, she is an extraordinarily beautiful woman. Just as you are yourself, but somehow I think you will never be quite as aware of it as she. I expect that flirtation comes to her as naturally as breathing. If she were to do it and you were to ask her a minute later, she would not know about it. Indeed, if she has only *possibly* made herself a flirt in the little time you have known her, I think she is acting with great restraint."

"How very glad I am to have you here," Louisa said very seriously. "You put things in a proper perspective. You always did. I have made some very unwise decisions lately, acted in an overconfident way and reaped the consequences."

"Tell me something to surprise me," Miss Patterson reported.

"Well then, I will," Louisa exclaimed. "I have met two of the most unusual people. Their name is Rioux. They are brother and sister. And French, although brought up in England. They live next door, and they moved there for the purpose of making my acquaintance in order that I might introduce them to some members of the *haut ton*. Some very particular members: people who are secretly in the pay of Napoleon, who send him information. You see the Riouxes are spies!"

She said it all in a great rush, and Miss Patterson shook her head and frowned. "You were always headstrong, my dear, and it seems nothing has changed. A little independence is one thing. In fact, I like a young lady to show a deal of spirit. That was one of the first things I told your father when he brought me to you ten years ago. But spies, my dear! I'm sure I do not know."

"I think that Papa would approve what I am doing," she replied, and added, in an effort to turn the conversation to one side: "He always said he could not fault my education. You should hear him praise you."

"Even though he knows about the Suetonius I let you read?" the headmistress asked, distracted. "All that Roman scandal. And Fielding and the other writers? There are a good many fathers who would not think such . . . classical breadth desirable for their daughters."

"Papa does not think anything you taught me was wrong," Louisa answered. "He always put his trust in you absolutely. And he has perfect judgment."

To Louisa's considerable surprise, she saw Miss Patterson blush. And, somehow, that made her remember that every time her father had visited the school, he had made a point of engaging the headmistress in private discussions which he seemed particularly to enjoy.

"Well, then," Miss Patterson replied, "you must trust his judgment in regard to Lady Landor. He may not have known her long, but to my mind there could be nothing more calculated to reveal a person's character than a rough voyage on the Bay of Biscay."

In the midst of another fit of laughter, Louisa made a sudden decision. "You must agree to stay here," she declared, sweeping the headmistress to her feet. "Come. You *must* agree. I need you. And I know that Lady Landor would be delighted, for it was clear she liked you. How long will your business keep you in London?"

For once Miss Patterson seemed disconcerted. "Why, since it is between terms at school, perhaps a week or two," she said. "But I could not impose . . ."

"Oh, but you could," Louisa told her gayly. "I need you, as I have said before. Only consider the matter of the spies who live next door."

Miss Patterson's black eyes sparkled over the gold-rimmed spectacles which, as usual, had slipped down to the very tip of her snub nose. "Well then, I shall," she said. "There is nothing I should enjoy more. I have always wanted to be in the center of intrigue of one sort or another. And it seems you can provide it in various varieties, my dear."

Nothing would do but Lady Landor must be called at once and, as Louisa had supposed, she was delighted at the proposal. She was still in her dressing gown since it was not yet noon, but she was as lushly beautiful as though she were attired for a ball, and as she took Miss Patterson's hands in welcome, Louisa thought of what a strange contrast they made, the headmistress neat in gray, with her gold spectacles and pulled-back hair which, when she wore her bonnet, was completely hidden, and Lady Landor with her mass of chestnut curls and liquid eyes. And yet, ironically, the girl realized for the first time, Miss Patterson's features were regular enough to be lovely, except for the retroussé nose which lent an air of pertness to the face, or would have done so if it were not for those spectacles. Louisa wondered if the headmistress really needed them, for if she did, why were they always slipping down her nose? And what a difference it would make if her dark hair could be pulled loose from its chignon.

But these were idle musings. Louisa knew full well that, although a week or two of London intrigue might amuse Miss Patterson, her heart was with her school, her students, and her books. Once she had confided in the girl that this was the height of her ambition.

"I have always wanted to be independent," she had said. "My mother had no life of her own, you see. There were the children. One each year almost. And she seemed to think it one of nature's laws that she should be at the beck and call of my father every minute of her life. When my uncle offered to adopt me, give me an education, nothing could have kept me from him. And when he died and left me the money for the school, I felt the most fortunate woman in the world. And I still do."

Had she never had a lover, Louisa wondered now. Certainly she was broad-minded, at least when it came to literature. And, in agreeing to stay here in the face of slander, she was demonstrating a liberal quality in her nature. Certainly she was not about to hasten to condemn Lady Landor, as were so many others. Best of all, in Louisa's opinion, was the fact that Miss Patterson shared her own conviction that her father's judgment could not be faulted.

"What a good time we shall have," Lady Landor was saying, taking the hand of each and whirling them about, as though they all were children. "We will ride out this afternoon, the three of us, in The Mall. You will wear white muslin, Louisa, and look as demure as you can be. And Miss Patterson is perfect in gray merino, and I . . ."

"You will be quite proper, too," Louisa murmured.

" Oh, well," Lady Landor said with a toss of her head, "I suppose I shall. What a comfort it is to have my friends about me. And now I will go and have Maria dress my hair and help me find a gown."

Chapter Twelve

THE Duchess of Taxton was one of the most exclusive hostesses in London. That was clear, Louisa thought, from the moment that the two liveried footmen, perfectly matched as to height and coloring, threw open the great double doors which opened onto a vast hall floored with marble. But it was not the house which told her that her hostess was one of the most prestigious members of the *haut ton*. Rather it was the manner and the dress of the people about her. Almack's had been her introduction to the *haut ton*, and she could see now that, taken in its broader sense, that element of society included a vast range of members who had in common only money, a title, or as was the case with Beau Brummell, a reputation.

Here, however, there were gathered only people of the more cultured sort. Something in the way they carried themselves and talked proclaimed a certain elegance. In a word, it was not the sort of gathering which could have easily absorbed someone as vulgar as Lady Ellis and her daughters or, for that matter, Sir Thomas Tigger with his store of scandal.

"How kind it was of the Duchess to invite me," Miss Patterson observed as, together with Lady Landor and Louisa, she walked along a carpeted path leading to the winding stairs, which in turn led to the second story where the drawing room was located. "It was kind of her to invite your French friends, as well. I hope I will have a chance to meet them this evening."

Louisa wished the schoolmistress had not reminded her that Michelle and Claude Rioux would be on hand. It had all been a mistake from the beginning; whereas she had been perfectly willing to introduce them and see invitations sent out to them for general affairs, she had not wanted them included in a party such as this: not because she thought it too exclusive in the social sense, nor because she was à snob, but because the people the duchess would have here were beyond suspicion. None of them could have been involved in giving information to Napoleon. And yet, indirectly, Louisa had been responsible, since Claire had spoken to the duchess about them as being attractive and friends of Louisa.

"I know you have few friends, as yet, in London," the duchess had written. "And so I mean to include Mademoiselle Rioux and her brother."

Since there had been nothing she could do to prevent it, Louisa had contented herself with writing a note to Michelle, warning her that they would see no one of the sort they were looking for at that particular party, and it was little use their going. Michelle, however, had written in reply that neither Claude nor she would dream of missing the affair and that they were more grateful to Louisa for arranging it than either of them could say.

"We must hurry in order to be in the reception line in time to greet the first guests," Lady Landor remarked over her shoulder. "It was my fault that we were not here before, and I shall tell the Duchess that straight away. Oh, dear! I am so terribly nervous. That was why I changed my mind about my gown at the last minute. Maria is a jewel. She did not even frown though she had done up a hundred buttons. Oh, dear! I knew I should stumble on this little train. I should have settled on a shorter hem all around."

Still talking, she outdistanced them, and Louisa, pausing to catch her breath, saw her take the duchess's hand at the entrance to the grand salon and continue to talk in her rapid pace, presumably explaining again about the changing of the gown.

"I think that she looks very lovely," Miss Patterson said with a smile. "Do you agree?"

Louisa nodded. "You must take the credit," she told the headmistress. "How clever of you to convince her that she looked regal in pale lavender and that, by using that Brussels lace about her bodice, she succeeded in teasing the imagination instead of gratifying it straight away."

"My dear Louisa," Miss Patterson replied, pretending to be shocked. "I hope I did not put it in quite such a vulgar way. But I admit it does become her to be modest. As for the hair, we reached a compromise. It troubles her to hide it, you understand, even though she *is* a matron, and turbans are indicated. But she told me that it was her crowning glory and that she did not intend to hide it away."

"At least she allowed Maria to wrap a silver bandeau about it," Louisa said. "Yes, you are right. She *is* lovely. No wonder my father was attracted."

"She has other excellent qualities, as well," the headmistress declared quite firmly. "She is extraordinarily good natured."

"But perhaps not too intelligent?"

"Intelligence!" Miss Patterson exclaimed. "It is difficult enough to measure it in a school, let alone when the lady in question is one's hostess who has done everything she could to make herself agreeable. Perhaps she does not read books. Still, that is no proof . . . Now, what sort of tangent have you got me off on? You will want to join the reception line, as well."

"No," Louisa said as she followed the headmistress up the stairs. "I told the Duchess that I wanted this to be Lady Landor's evening, with no distractions."

"Well, as for that," the older woman told her, "I think a few heads will be turned for your sake. That ivory silk was an inspiration. And those tiny sleeves show off your neck and arms to best advantage. Indeed, you have already attracted the attention of one young man. Why, I do not believe he has taken his eyes off you since we started up the stairs."

Looking up, Louisa said Lord Cardross. He was wearing evening dress, and his dark eyes had never seemed more intense.

"Why, my dear, he is very handsome," Miss Patterson said behind her fan. She was neatly outfitted in a dark blue chemise with the hem cut as long as fashion would allow and tight sleeves to her wrists. At Louisa's pleading, she had left off her spectacles, but she had refused to change the mode in which she wore her hair and, as a consequence, still managed to look severe. "Will you introduce me to him?"

Louisa knew that she was flushing. "How can you be so certain that I know him?" she retorted.

"Well, my dear," Miss Patterson said calmly, "either you know him now or you very shortly will. I have been hibernating in a school for girls for a good many years—twelve to be exact—but that does not mean I do not know how to interpret an expression in a gentleman's eyes."

Louisa thought that, in the past, she had given the headmistress credit for a good many things but not for such telling observation. And yet in this case she was wrong. But there was no opportunity to tell her, for Lord Cardross was no more than an arm's length away now, and they must make room for other people coming up the stairs.

"Miss Rogers," he said, making a bow. "My best wishes for the evening. I hope it will be a great success."

That, Louisa thought, was a suitably formal greeting to warn Miss Patterson that she must expect no great degree of intimacy to be shown. But, of course, there was no need to fear that by a single word the headmistress would disappoint or embarrass her. Indeed, she allowed herself to be introduced with great aplumb, declaring that she had heard a great deal of his mother and something of his sister, and that she was glad that Louisa had made such excellent friendships. It was then that Louisa revealed that Lord Cardross was her father's friend.

"I am glad to hear it, sir," the headmistress said. "He is a gentleman a young man like yourself might emulate to advantage. Good heavens, how very stilted I sound. No use to try to hide my profession, I imagine. And now, I expect, we must go through the receiving line and see how Lady Landor is faring."

She was as natural as though she attended a soiree such as this every evening, Louisa marveled, and she was glad to see that Lord Cardross apparently saw how remarkable she was.

"A woman who knows herself," he said in a low voice, as Louisa preceded him to the grand salon. "Your father told me once that ladies are not made but born. I think he must have had your Miss Patterson in mind."

Thus the evening opened delightfully. Lady Landor, her splendor somewhat subdued thanks to lavender silk and Brussels lace, stood beside the duchess and welcomed everyone in her cheerful way. Surely, Louisa thought as she stood watching her, no one who met her tonight could pay attention to anything that either Lady Ellis or Sir Thomas had to say. What a relief it was to think that by the time her father returned to London his bride-to-be would have been settled comfortably in society. Never had Louisa wanted more to see him happy.

Since fifty people would have rattled about the grand ballroom, according to Claire, who appeared, sparkling in pink silk, on Hugh Trever's arm, the duchess had chosen to have musicians play in the blue salon.

"Very much like something out of the Arabian Nights," Miss Patterson commented, looking pleased. "I was afraid your duchess might be stuffy, my dear, but she reminds me of a sparrow who is as interested as can be in everything around. As for the Duke, it seems clear to me that he would rather be drinking claret in his library. When we came through the line she told me that it was all she could do to get him to play host, but that no one was to mind."

The duchess had ordered waltzes to be played, since she did not share the general reservation about that propriety. "You and Miles made quite a picture, my dear," she said to Louisa later when the reception line had been abandoned. "You look quite lovely in that silk. And I do like your Miss Patterson. I told her that she should not sit with the matrons along the wall. But she told me that she preferred to watch. Oh dear! Where can the Duke have disappeared? I expect that I will have to send one of the footmen to the library to rout him out."

Louisa danced the next waltz with a young marquess who flirted with her outrageously. And then, although she thought she saw Lord Cardross heading in her direction, a Mr. Williams, who was something at the bar, claimed her for the third. It was while she was being swung about the room on this occasion that she noticed Miss Patterson in Lord Cardross's arms. The sight of her headmistress with her neck bent back and laughing took Louisa so much by surprise that she nearly missed a step.

She actually did miss another when she saw her French neighbors at the other end of the room. They were not together, but they both stood out in their natural elegance. Michelle was slim and beautiful in white silk, dancing with someone Louisa did not know, a gentleman who was talking away at a great rate while Michelle listened very closely. As for Claude, his partner was an older woman who was equally garrulous while he was just as attentive as his sister. What sort of information were they gathering, Louisa wondered? She hoped, at this occasion, it was nothing. Suddenly, she wished that they had not come into her life. But later, when Michelle and her partner passed her and Mr. Williams and greetings were exchanged, there was nothing for Louisa to do but be gracious. The damage—if there were damage—had been done.

So distracted was she that she nearly forgot to watch for Lady Landor. That afternoon she and Miss Patterson had had a private talk from which Lady Landor had emerged with a thoughtful look that might or might not explain why she behaved with so much modesty, not refusing dances, but behaving decorously both on and off the dance floor. On one occasion, Louisa saw her dancing with the Duke of Taxton whom the duchess had evidently forced onto the floor. This apparently being a challenge Lady Landor could not resist, she was being more amusing than she had ever been before and to very good effect, for the duke was soon set to laughing heartily at something which she said, and he even managed, simultaneously, to dip and turn to the beat the musicians made.

It was not until the dancing broke for supper, which was served in the dining room downstairs, that Louisa caught another glimpse of Lord Cardross. This time he lost no time in hastening to her side and declared it his intention to take her down to supper if she was not otherwise engaged.

With unspoken consent, they lingered behind the others and watched the musicians put their violins away and retreat down the back staircase, presumably to the kitchen where they, too, would be refreshed. Empty, the grand salon seemed even more impressive than when it was full of people, its columns that ran down both sides topped with Corinthian capitals with their wealth of scroll work, the walls between painted a midnight blue that matched the velvet of the drapes. Some of the windows were open, it being a mild evening, and the candles, which glittered by the scores in the two grand chandeliers, flickered in the little breezes which came and went.

For a moment they made idle conversation. Lady Landor, he agreed, was showing herself to remarkable good effect. "Everyone I have heard speaking of her has said that she is charming," he said in a low voice, his dark eyes tracing the fine lines of her face. "No one here tonight is ill bred enough to speak openly of any scandal, but it is clear that they are relieved to find her to be guileless and full of grace. I think we can be certain that your father will not return to London to find her in an alienated state. This evening will result in many invitations of the best sort, I promise you."

"All thanks to your mother who introduced us to the Duchess who was generous enough to create tonight," Louisa said with a lighter heart than she had felt for days.

But they had not, it seemed, lingered behind the others simply for the purpose of congratulation. "I will not be able to go on with the business we spoke of the other day," he told her, his face darkening. "By that I mean that soon I must go away."

Strange, how violently the words affected her. Louisa felt something drop inside her and waited, silent, for his explanation.

For surely he would give one. People did not simply go away. There was always a reason. Perhaps he meant to go into the country. There must be an estate. Some urgent business which his agent could not manage . . . .

"I am not certain when I will be called," she heard him saying. "The message might come at any moment. Still, that is not important as far as you are concerned except that I will not be able to go about finding someone who has been in Florence, someone who can counter everything that Sir Thomas Tigger has said about the lady your father means to marry."

Accustomed as she was to sudden goings and comings because of her father's military occupations, Louisa still was taken aback. But, before she could speak, Lord Cardross continued.

"Some word should be in London when I return," he said. "I have written certain letters. Some abroad and others not. The latter may be waiting for me. I only urge you not to bring the sayings of either Lady Ellis or Sir Thomas to your father if he should be back in London before I am. No good can come from it, and I am afraid that he would try to defend Lady Landor's honor, as I said before."

"Have you some reason to think that he will soon be with us?" Louisa asked him.

For a moment he hesitated, and then, avoiding the question entirely, he went on. "You may not want advice of me, Miss Rogers," he told her. "But I will give it all the same. You must prepare yourself, quite privately, for the eventuality that some of what scandal has been spread about Lady Landor may be true."

She stared at him, astounded. "But your mother does not think that!" she exclaimed. "Neither does the Duchess nor all the people who have come here tonight."

"They prefer not to think the worst, particularly when the worst is bandied about as it is. I only say that you must not be too disillusioned if some of it is true. Some part of you must remain quite apart from—from all of this. Do you understand me? Society, even the politest, is a jungle. Ah, you smile at that. You think that I exaggerate. Only ask your Miss Patterson. I think she can explain just what I mean."

He drew closer, and his eyes were hooded. "There is another thing," he told her. "Your French friends are here tonight. I will not mention now whether or not what you have done is wise. I only warn you that you may see little of them in the near future.

They may appear to vanish. But say nothing. Above all, tell no one what you are doing for them. What you *have* done, I should say, for it may well be they will not call on you again.''

Louisa stared at him. "What do you know of my relations with them?" she demanded. "And why should they appear to vanish? There is no need for mystery. . . ."

"Oh, but perhaps there is, Miss Rogers," he told her. "And now I think we are expected downstairs."

He was so clearly determined to say nothing more that there was nothing Louisa could do except accompany him to the great dining room, where creams and jellies were being served along with other delicacies. Lady Landor was sitting beside the duke, intent on making him laugh between bites of oyster patties, while Miss Patterson was close in conversation with Claire and Hugh. As for Louisa and Lord Cardross, they were scarely seated when a footman came to him, carrying a letter on a silver salver.

Something in Louisa told her, even before he spoke, that it was the message he had been waiting for, the message that would take him away. Louisa watched in bitter silence as he made his excuses and strode out the door.

"It is nothing to be concerned about," Claire told her carelessly. "Miles is always going away on some business or other."

But Louisa noticed that, even though Lady Cardross said the same, there was a worried frown between her eyes and that she winced at the sound, in the distance, of the closing of the door.

Chapter Thirteen

"I believe that the most common word used in your regard was charming," Miss Patterson declared the next morning over breakfast. "Charming and gracious. Quite the best combination, really."

"La, do you think so?" Lady Landor replied, pouting her lips. "I mean to say, I have always preferred to be called beautiful and exciting. Charming and gracious sound so very . . ."

"Mature," Miss Patterson said firmly, as Lady Landor groped for words. "You are a girl no longer, madam, and you must solicit descriptions which reflect your dignity."

"My dignity!" Lady Landor exclaimed. "Why, I do declare, I never thought of myself as having any. By that I do not mean I ever wanted to be undignified, precisely, but . . ."

"Mature dignity," Miss Patterson told her, as though by repeating the words she could impress the point on Lady Landor's mind. Louisa, who had often seen the headmistress employ this technique with recalcitrant students, pressed a napkin to her lips to hide a smile. "You must be thought elegant and not exotic, lovely and not glorious, gentle and not gay. You must build the proper image and live up to it, just as you did last night."

It was strange, Louisa thought, although not completely unpredictable, that Lady Landor should so quickly have come to regard the headmistress as her mentor. Although they were much the same age, Miss Patterson carried the heritage of the classroom with her which gave her words an added weight.

She had not volunteered advice, Louisa noted. Oh, no. She was far too clever for that. But, in describing her conception of Lady Landor's success, she had heard so many words that Captain Roger's bride-to-be had never heard applied to herself, that respectful attention had been commanded, and now, Louisa thought,

93

she had settled in the palm of Miss Patterson's hand, as so many others had before, and was waiting to be instructed.

"The lavender gown was so becoming," Miss Patterson was saying now. "I heard a number of ladies comment on it. One of them said that if she were you she would never wear another color. Bright shades war with your hair and sometimes overcome it."

Lady Landor leaned her chin on the palm of her hand and looked at the headmistress with rapt attention. "I never thought of it like that," she said as thoughtfully as though she were solving a complicated mathematical problem. "Of course it is my best feature. My hair, I mean."

Saying which, she pulled a strand of it over her shoulder and surveyed its chestnut perfection with a natural pride which displayed itself in a fond smile.

"Speaking of your hair," Miss Patterson went on, sipping her tea, "it could not have been shown to better effect than it was last night, bound with a bandeau."

"I always thought that when I let it stream over my shoulders . . ." Lady Landor began.

"That was very well when you were a girl," the headmistress told her.

"Oh dear," Lady Landor pouted. "That is how I always think of myself, you know. Perhaps it comes from having been made a bride so early. And then dear Alfred told me that I should never change. He loved me as a girl, and he said nothing about me should *ever* change."

"I am sure you made him very happy," Miss Patterson replied. "But those days are to be put behind you now, I think."

Lady Landor considered the suggestion with a seriousness which was itself delightful. "It would be a challenge to me," she said doubtfully. "To be dignified, I mean. I declare I am not certain that I should know how to set about it. Unless, of course, you would agree to help me."

And she looked at Miss Patterson with the same appeal which had characterized the way she had looked at Mr. Trever that other morning.

"Why, as for that," the headmistress said, suddenly confused, "it would be my pleasure to assist you."

"You must be her mentor," Louisa declared. "She could ask for no one better. And," she added in a lower voice, "you know how much it means."

THE IVORY FAN

In the silence that followed, the sound of the knocker falling on its brass plate on the door was heard.

"Dear me, the invitations are already beginning to arrive," Lady Landor exclaimed.

Louisa and Miss Patterson exchanged a puzzled glance. It was too early for callers in the ordinary way, and neither of them shared Lady Landor's hope that invitations would stream in in torrents despite the fact that the evening before could be counted as a success. In fact, in order for such messages to arrive so early, the hostesses in question must needs have been up betimes.

As all three ladies sat in expectation, the footman came into the morning room and announced, in his expressionless way, that Captain Rogers was in the drawing room.

"Papa!" Louisa exclaimed.

"Robert!" Lady Landor cried.

Only Miss Patterson said nothing, although the color drained from her thin cheeks.

"Only let me have a moment alone with him," Lady Landor declared, throwing down her napkin and starting to her feet. Regardless of the fact that she was in her dressing gown, she flung herself out of the sunny room and down the hall, with the footman following a respectful distance after.

"But why are you so pale?" Louisa demanded. "You knew that he might return at any moment. How glad I will be to see him, although I confess that I would be easier in my mind if you had had the opportunity to counsel her further in matters of decorum."

The headmistress sat very straight in her chair. "It occurs to me that that will be a problem," she said in a low voice. "What right have I to help her to change what she is?"

"Why, every right," Louisa told her. "It was she who asked you. Just now she asked you. And it was thanks to you she made such a good impression last night at the Duchess's soiree."

"Yes, but don't you see?" Miss Patterson said with more urgency than Louisa had ever seen her express before. "It came to me quite suddenly that it might have been the most dreadful mistake if I had had time to help her change before your father returned. He expects to see her as she is. He fell in love with her as she is. The Duke, her former husband, did not want her to change, and why should your father be different?"

So that explained the sudden paleness, Louisa thought. Miss Patterson had been quite right to characterize her as headstrong,

95

for she had never thought of that part of it. Her father had, indeed, met a flamboyant creature during that romantic passage across the Bay of Biscay. He had seen her childlike, lacking dignity. For all Louisa knew, she might even have flirted with the sailors, or at least the ship captain. That was the person her father had given his heart to, not a dignified personage dressed in lavender with her chestnut curls nearly hidden by a bandeau.

"But when he discovers the trouble her appearance has caused her here in London," she began, "when he understands that the way she dresses and conducts herself only lends fuel to the rumors . . ."

"He must know nothing of the rumors," the headmistress warned her. "If, that is, we can prevent it."

She was right, Louisa thought, as she and Miss Patterson hurried to the drawing room, right on every count. How complicated everything might be. She found herself wishing that Lord Cardross had not been called away on some mysterious errand. He could have offered good advice and, besides, he was her father's friend.

They found the happy couple standing in the center of the Oriental drawing room. Captain Rogers was a tall, handsome man with grizzled hair, who wore his green coat and buckskin breeches with a flare. It came to Louisa to wonder why he was not in uniform, but the thought was dashed away by his embrace.

"I thought that I would take you by surprise," he said against her cheek. "There is nothing better than to see that one has really been missed. Why then, Miss Patterson! This is an unexpected pleasure, to be sure. I did not know you ever strayed quite so far from the academy."

"She is here to teach me to be dignified, Robert, my dear," Lady Landor exclaimed before Louisa could stop her. "But we will talk about all that later. You must tell us all about your adventures. Come, sit here beside me. No secrets, mind!"

It occurred to Louisa that Lady Landor knew even less about her father than the brief length of their courtship might have led her to believe. As long as she had known her father, he had never once told her anything of his military activities, except, on occasion, where he had been.

"Any stories I might have to tell would be tiresome in the extreme," he said now, turning aside her questions gently. "What I want to hear about is your reception here in London. Have you and Louisa been burning candles at both ends?"

Fortunately for Louisa, Lady Landor gave her no time to answer. "Why, as for that," she told him, "we were entertained last night by no one less than the Duchess of Taxton and her husband. It was an exclusive gathering, or so I am told by Lady Cardross. It was at her house that we met the Duchess, and both of them have been so very kind. Otherwise, we have only been to Almack's, which was rather strange. I mean to say that people stared and . . ."

"Lord Cardross was there," Louisa said in desperation, saying the first thing which came to mind. "He said that you and he were friends."

"Miles is an excellent fellow," Captain Rogers declared, apparently distracted from the implications of what Lady Landor had said. "No doubt I will see him today when I drop in at White's."

"I am afraid that he was called away from town last evening, Papa," Louisa told him, hoping to keep the conversation on a safer course.

To her surprise, her father frowned. "Ah, I was afraid of that," he muttered. "No matter. I will see him when he returns."

"He paid a marked attention to Louisa, I thought," Lady Landor said in her excited fashion. "But then, of course, she danced with this one and that and was quite the belle, I thought. Do you not agree, Miss Patterson?"

Captain Rogers turned to the headmistress with his thick eyebrows raised in an expression of surprise. "Why, did you attend the Duchess's soiree, as well, madam?" he said. "I am glad to hear it, but it comes as a surprise."

"You do not think a London salon quite my milieu, sir?" the headmistress said with a slow smile, and Louisa thought that no doubt, she, too, was hoping to carry the conversation as far distant as possible from Lady Landor's mention of her reception at Almack's.

"I think that you should do very well in a salon, as in a classroom," Captain Rogers told her with the familiarity which he showed to his oldest friends.

And, in a strange way, that was precisely what they were, Louisa thought. For the past ten years he had come regularly to the academy to visit her, and on every occasion, he and Miss Patterson had found the time to walk and talk together, about her, no doubt. About the child without a mother.

Miss Patterson had never attempted to be that, Louisa recalled. And yet there must have been a temptation, because there had been an affinity between them from the start, an affinity that the head-mistress had clearly not felt for any of the other girls. Not only had they shared the love of the same literature, but Louisa had been a constant presence at the academy. She had come to love the academy's rambling brick Georgian building as completely as though it really had been her home. Holidays had sometimes been spent with her father somewhere at a spa, but more often his military business had taken him away from England. Some of her happiest memories had been of her and Miss Patterson, roaming the sunken lanes ablaze with poppies. And reading.

How different it all was now. In London. Living, as she was, with an extravagant-hearted woman who was unlike anyone she had ever known. How good it was to feel that, for a week or two, at least, Miss Patterson would be a moderating influence, someone who would not let her forget that there were values other than those provided by the *haut ton*.

"Miss Patterson says that I look very well in lavender," Lady Landor was saying now. "That was the color of the gown I wore last night. It gave me dignity. Is that not amusing, my dear Robert? Here. Only wait and I will give a demonstration of the new sort of lady I intend to become."

And, with that, she hurried out of the room, her brocade dressing gown billowing about her. How shocked Mrs. Thrasher would be, Louisa thought, to know that Lady Landor had entertained her intended in dishabille. *And*, that his daughter and a schoolmistress had been in attendance! It was not, the girl imagined, the ordinary thing at all. And yet it had not appeared to disconcert her father, who now turned his full attention to her.

"Does London please you?" he asked her. "And are you fond of Lady Landor? I was certain that you would make excellent companions, for sometimes she scarcely seems older than you, my dear Louisa."

If the truth were told, Louisa thought, she herself probably seemed the elder, but of that she said nothing. Yes, of course she was happy. Particularly since he had made his return. And no one could have been kinder to her than Lady Landor. And if there were other matters troubling her, this was not the time to mention them, if ever. She wondered if, when Lord Cardross had warned her not to speak of Michelle and Claude Rioux to anyone, he had meant to include her father, as well.

"But what is all this about her being taught dignity?" Captain Rogers was asking Miss Patterson. "'Pon my soul, she passed over it so quickly that I was not at all certain what she could mean."

"Oh, it is nothing, sir. Nothing," the headmistress replied. "Lady Landor is considering a certain change in her demeanor. Her appearance. What you will! But no doubt you like her very well just as she is. If so, you must tell her."

"But of course I like her as she is," Captain Rogers said with a bemused look. "Why on earth should I not? Clearly she has made herself comfortable in society and that is the important thing. After we are married, I would like to think she was never lonely. And, of course, my dear Louisa, there is you to see to. Can you think of anyone better prepared to see to your coming out?"

Louisa, not certain of just where to look, saw the expression in Miss Patterson's dark eyes and realized, all of the sudden, that the headmistress was in love with her father and that the pain which this discussion had given her was scarcely to be believed.

Chapter Fourteen

WHEN Captain Rogers announced that they would all celebrate by attending Almack's that evening, Lady Landor was ecstatic but it was all that Louisa could do to hide her doubts.

"Your father has always been a very social gentleman," Miss Patterson reminded her when they were alone in Louisa's bed chamber. "It is only to be expected that he would want to show his bride-to-be off to the world, to have all his friends see them in company together."

Louisa was sitting at her dressing table, letting her friend comb her black curls. How strange it was, she thought, that now they were no longer student and headmistress they could be even closer than they had been before. She knew that she must never let the older woman know that she had guessed her secret. How long, Louisa wondered, had Miss Patterson felt as she did about the dashing captain who had come to her school so many times over the years with his only purpose to talk of the daughter whom she was raising for him. For that had been the way of it, Louisa told herself. No mother could have watched over her more carefully than the headmistress even though, being the same age as Lady Landor, she was too young really to have performed that office.

Closing her eyes, Louisa relaxed under Miss Patterson's gentle touch. Would it be cruel of her to urge her to remain? When she had first agreed to stay and help with Lady Landor, there had been no thought that the captain would make such a sudden return. Louisa's mind drifted to Lord Cardross, as it so often seemed to do, and remembered something he had said the evening of his departure about her father coming back to England soon, and that thought led straight on to another. Why had her father frowned when he had heard that Lord Cardross was gone? Was it simply because he was disappointed that he would not see him? Perhaps so. At all events, it would do her no good to speculate.

"I know that it is only natural that he should want to go to Almack's," Louisa said now, returning to the subject at hand. "There is no way in the world I can dissuade him, outside of telling him the straight truth, and that I do not want to do."

She opened her eyes and met Miss Patterson's direct gaze in the mirror. How much did it hurt her, Louisa wondered, to see her father and Lady Landor together? How difficult was it for her to concentrate on their problem? How much loss did she feel? Surely she could never have expected anything to come of their brief meetings. And yet, who knows what may have passed between them on the walks they had taken or during the winter evenings when they had sat together by candlelight close to the fire in the headmistress's study.

"There may be no need to worry," Miss Patterson told her, putting down the comb. "Some of the fifty people who were at the Duchess's entertainment yesterday evening are certain to be at Almack's tonight, and they will not snub her."

"But others will," Louisa fretted. "Lady Ellis for one. Do you think she will be able to resist the opportunity to make a point of her disapproval in front of my father? Why, it is the chance she has been waiting for. And what about Sir Thomas Tigger? What a perfect opportunity for him to provide some humiliation. I declare I do not think it could be worse! And what are we to do about it?"

Miss Patterson crossed the room and stood at one of the long windows overlooking the square. As usual, the gold-rimmed spectacles had slipped down on her nose, and she was wearing an expression Louisa recognized as one she sometimes assumed when she was dealing with a problem that would not lend itself to an easy solution.

"I wonder if I should stay here," she said at last in a low voice, almost as though she were speaking to herself.

"But you must!" Louisa exclaimed, starting up from her seat by the dressing table. She was wearing a white muslin frock caught high above her waist with ribbon, and the scoop of neckline, thanks to Lady Landor's dressmaker, was so fashionably wide that her loose curls fell on her bare shoulders, giving her the look of an even younger girl. "I would not know what to do without you just now. Besides, why shouldn't you stay. Father thinks so much of you and . . ."

She stopped herself, realizing that she had blundered into forbidden territory. It could only give the schoolmistress pain to be reminded that she had Captain Rogers's high regard. Louisa forced herself to admit to herself, at least, that the situation was one in which, were Miss Patterson to stay, she would be wounded over and over again. Tonight, for example, should she really be expected to stand with Louisa in the hall and watch the dashing captain greet his exotic bride-to-be? Should she be put to the misery of watching the man she loved proudly enter Almack's with Lady Landor on his arm? It would be out of the question, clearly, under any other circumstances but those which made it all too probable that Lady Landor would be met with hostility in some quarters, a hostility which would leave Captain Rogers confused. Someone would have to explain it to him, and Louisa confessed to wanting Miss Patterson by her side.

"I hate to leave you like this, however," the headmistress said, as though her thoughts had paralleled Louisa's own. "There is certain to be trouble. If only he had come back later . . .''

And she put her finger to her lip and considered deeply as though faced by some problem in mathematics. Louisa found herself wishing that they were both back again in the safety of the academy with its brick walls covered thick with ivy and larks rising from the hills about. Perhaps that was why Miss Patterson had chosen the life she had. Donned the gold-rimmed spectacles. Drawn her fine black hair back in a knot. Been parent, teacher, friend to other people's children. More than friend to one.

"If you want to leave us," Louisa said in a low voice, "I shall understand."

Miss Patterson looked at her and, seeing something she had not expected in the girl's eyes, flushed.

"I—I only want you and your father to be happy," she said, and then added stiffly, as though facing an unruly class: "All in all it will be better if I leave you. My advice may not be right and, were you or anyone to act on it and come to trouble, I would never forgive myself. My advice to Lady Landor to the effect that she act and dress in a more dignified manner is a case in point. Clearly your father likes her just as she is."

"When he knows everything," Louisa told her, "he will see the need for her to assume new habits as clearly as we do."

"Well," Miss Patterson said with a sigh, "do you mean to tell him? Or will you let him find out on his own about the rumors?"

Louisa bit her lip. "If I tell him," she said finally, "he may well challenge Sir Thomas. Lord Cardross warned me of that."

"Do you think there is a possibility of keeping it from him?" the headmistress asked her. "If we both were to try to keep people like Lady Ellis and those who believe her stories away from him tonight at Almack's, no doubt Claire and her mother and the Duchess and . . ."

"And Mr. Trever!" Louisa interrupted. "He would be glad to help us, I know. It might work. We could try it. Besides, Papa is popular. It might be that even people who have listened to the scandal and half believe it will go out of their way to be pleasant to Lady Landor on his account."

And so it was decided, without a further word being said specifically on the subject, that Miss Patterson would remain and assist in making Captain Rogers's first public appearance with Lady Landor as much of a success as it could be. Notes were written to the Cardross and Taxton households and, within the hour, back came replies from Lady Cardross and Claire, each declaring themselves allies in the affair.

"To be frank, I had not intended to go to Almack's tonight," Lady Cardross had written, "but now, you can depend upon it. I will be among the first to greet your father and Lady Landor with enthusiasm, Miss Rogers. Claire is writing you to the same effect, I know, and she will, of course, talk to Hugh. I hope that you have written to the Duchess. The Duke cannot be depended on, I fear, since, to my certain knowledge, he has never set foot in Almack's nor any other place, for that matter, where whist is never played. Keep your spirits high, my dear, for I am certain that all will be well. Your father is liked and admired in many quarters, you know, and that in itself may make all the difference."

Much encouraged, Louisa and Miss Patterson broke the seal of the Duchess of Taxton's letter and discovered that, not only did she intend to put in an appearance, but that, when informed of what was brewing, the duke himself had declared that he would not miss the opportunity of helping to set things right for the delightful lady he had met the evening before.

"I have never seen him so impressed by anyone," the duchess had written, "all of which would leave me green with envy if I was not so glad to have him rouse himself a bit after all these years of avoiding any company without cards in their hands. If Lady Landor's presence is sufficient to lure him to Almack's, good enough for her! At all events, never fear. We are all your friends now, as well as your father's, and we will present a united front."

As a consequence of the communications, Louisa was able to make her preparations for the evening with some degree of anticipation that all would go quite well. But, before she and Miss Patterson retired to make their own toilettes, they thought it the better part of wisdom to drop by Lady Landor's bedchamber and find out how she intended to outfit herself.

They found the lady curled on her chaise longue, watching Maria hold up first one gown and then the next. The extent of Lady Landor's wardrobe had never been so fully revealed to Louisa before, and she watched in wonder as the Italian maid, in her silent and dour way, drew out of the great mahogany wardrobe one gown after the next. Thanks to the current fashion, most of them were sheaths, loose over the bosom with a high waistline from which the skirt hung in soft drapes, with now and then a train to be carried over the arm. But there were also knee-length tunics, all of which had a fuller skirt beneath. Sleeves were either very short and puffed or long and tight, and these were all the differences in cut there were. But the colors and materials were extraordinarily varied, and there were quantities of outfits in a new, soft cloth called velvet and morning gowns in chintz. Among such a wealth of fashion, the plain lavender gown that Lady Landor had worn the night before did, indeed, look very sober.

"I had thought this morning that all of these must be thrown out," she told them excitedly, making room for Louisa on the chaise and flinging out one arm to indicate which chair Miss Patterson should take. "But now I shall keep them all, for when I asked your father if he wanted me to change, my dear Louisa, he said he certainly did not. Such a savings, really, I told him, although I do not think I made him understand. But some of these gowns I have not worn yet, and unless I hurry and do so, they will be quite out of fashion. No, Maria. I do not think that one will do. Bring out the scarlet satin. I love the way it clings. If one has a fine figure, one should show it, I always say. At least that was what Alfred always told me. He had an eye for figures, Alfred, despite his age. There now! What do you think of that one, Louisa? Try to smile, Maria, do!"

And, indeed, there was something incongruous about the dark, sullen gaze of the Italian abigail as she raised a green silk chemise gown in front of her for their appraisal. Louisa felt a stab of pity for Maria, here in a strange country whose language, thanks to years of serving Lady Landor, she could understand but either could or would not speak. That, in turn, made the girl think of the loneliness her father's intended must have suffered in Florence where she had been even more isolated by the restraints of language. If, as Sir Thomas Tigger suggested, she had sought friendships even more close than she had admitted in the English community, was it not perhaps to be forgiven?

But, if the scandal were true, would her father forgive this woman? Louisa could only hope that it would never come to that. If he truly loved Lady Landor, as he seemed to, she could not bear to have him hurt. Oh, what a strange thing life was, she reflected, glancing at Miss Patterson and thinking of her silent disappointment. Although, perhaps she had never dared to hope . . .

"What a wool gatherer you are today, Louisa," she heard Lady Landor cry. "I have just decided that I will wear the scarlet. But I am remembering what you said about the color warring with my hair, Miss Patterson. I shall overcome that difficulty by wearing a matching turban with three pink feathers in it. Do you think that will be a good idea?"

She was incorrigible, Louisa thought. And yet so full of charm. Clearly the headmistress did not mean to argue with her. After all, how could she, when Louisa's father had told the lady that he liked her as she was. And yet Louisa dreaded that moment when they would make their entrance at Almack's with Lady Landor resplendent in her scarlet gown. In her mind's eye, she could see Lady Ellis's eyes narrow and Mrs. Thrasher puff her indignation. It might be that all the efforts she and Lady Cardross and the others might expend would not be enough to prevent her father from seeing that the lady to whom he was affianced was creating quite another sort of sensation than the one he had in mind.

"There is something so innocent about her," Miss Patterson observed when they had left Lady Landor to the silent ministrations of Maria. "We must do everything we can to keep her and your father safe. You will think it fanciful of me, no doubt, but sometimes I see us all as the sort of cast Molière would have liked to gather for one of his comedies. If only there was not the underlying possibility of something tragic happening, I think that I could laugh."

"And this is the society in which I am supposed to make my life," Louisa mused. "Sometimes I think that I would rather follow your direction and . . ."

"No!" Miss Patterson said so sharply that Louisa gave a start. "If I chose to isolate myself—well, I had reasons. I will not let you be disillusioned. If we are very careful, this will all come right."

But Louisa thought her voice lacked conviction, and when they parted to make their preparations for the evening it was with a certain awkwardness on both their parts, an awkwardness that never had come between them in the past.

Chapter Fifteen

CAPTAIN Rogers had given Lady Landor an ivory fan, and she was holding it as she came down the stairs that evening.

"Your father knows how fond I am of everything Oriental," she told Louisa, "and this was made in China. Only think. There's not another like it in the world."

Both Louisa and Miss Patterson admired it, for it was truly a lovely thing, consisting as it did of slim, ivory panels carved with a relief of leaves and held together by bands of ribbon so that it could be folded into a single, precious sheath.

"I shall always carry it," Lady Landor declared in her usual extravagant manner. "Always! Louisa, you look lovely. And how well that dove gray becomes you, my dear Miss Patterson. We shall be a great success, I know. Now, if only Robert would oblige us by arriving with his carriage, we will be on our way to making a grand entrance."

Louisa wished that this last had not been said with so much relish, and was grateful when her father's carriage was heard outside. Captain Rogers, in evening dress, was even more handsome than usual, for he was a stylish man and employed one of the best tailors in London, preferring, unlike many other military gentlemen, to appear in civilian clothing when he was on the town. More than once it had occurred to Louisa to wonder how it was allowed, but her father had never encouraged her to ask questions about the army's rules and regulations and she thought that if he did receive special treatment it must be because of the nature of his assignments. Further than this speculation she never had cared to go.

With the exception of the fact that there were four instead of two of them, the evening began much as had the preceding visit to Almack's. King Street was as crowded as before, although Louisa noticed that their carriage was given way to and that they reached the hall with unusual dispatch. Furthermore, this time as they mingled with the others on the stairs, her father was so frequently greeted that it seemed everyone in London knew him. It was not the time or place for introductions, but it came to the girl that, once they reached the ballroom, her father could scarcely be prevented from taking Lady Landor about to meet a good many people. And some of them might show a certain distance. Even worse, those who believed the stories against her might turn away. Whereas she and Lady Cardross and the others might have some success in keeping Lady Ellis, Mrs. Thrasher, and Sir Thomas from him, they could not monitor his movements. A wave of anxiety swept over her as they made their entrance into the crowded ballroom.

Just as before, there was a sudden silence. Only this time it was worse because Louisa knew the reason for it. Fortunately her father put the wrong construction on the gaping mouths and staring faces.

"You have struck them down with your beauty, my dear," he said in a laughing voice to Lady Landor. "Or perhaps it is the scarlet gown."

Lady Landor smiled contentedly as one who liked nothing better than making a sensation, while Louisa and Miss Patterson exchanged wary glances. Both of them knew that the next few minutes were vital. Captain Rogers was too sensitive a man not to realize that he was mistaken if there was no immediate distraction.

And then, to their combined relief, they became the center of a little circle of chattering friends. Lady Cardross told Captain Rogers how glad she was to see him, and Claire offered him a kiss. Meanwhile, Hugh Trever and the duchess congratulated Lady Landor on her gown. But it was the Duke of Taxton, plump and portly, who delivered himself most expansively, much to everyone's surprise. The captain was a lucky fellow to have found himself such a prize, he declared with great conviction, and nothing would do but that he must shake his hand and offer best wishes all around.

To add to the general atmosphere of celebration, the orchestra struck up a merry tune and a country dance was announced. One of the young gentlemen Louisa had danced with at the duchess's soiree, a fine fellow with his hair done in the latest fashion, appeared to ask her to dance, but as soon as they were on the floor and the line was formed, Louisa saw that she had been too quickly lulled into the assurance that everything would be all right.

Keeping a stiff smile on her lips for the benefit of her partner as they moved down the line, Louisa saw that the enemy was advancing on Lady Landor from three corners of the room. Lady Ellis and her daughters were emerging from behind a column in a single file, much as though they were on military patrol. From the other side of the crowded room, briefly detached from between a moving camouflage of waving fans and towering piles of decorated hair, not to mention the shift and swing of quizzing glasses on their chains, she caught a glimpse of Sir Thomas Tigger, prancing along in her father's direction in his usual foppish fashion. Casting her eyes about, Louisa saw Mrs. Thrasher pushing her way through the crush with visible signs of exertion as her great bosom heaved and thrust its way before her.

There was, Louisa realized, very little she could do. The little group that had formed around her father and Lady Landor was still there, and an animated conversation was being carried on. No one looked in her direction as she was spun about in a whirl of embroidered muslin by the young man who was what was sometimes termed a vigorous performer on the dance floor. And then Miss Patterson looked up and caught Louisa's eye as the girl was spun past her.

Foregoing any attempts to pretend that she was attending to the figure that she was executing, Louisa pointed in three directions, leaving the young gentleman who was her partner to twirl about by himself for a few moments. At once the headmistress saw the danger and made no delay in gathering up resisting forces.

Everything was accomplished by whispers which the captain and Lady Landor did not notice, thanks to the vigor with which the Duke of Taxton was conducting his conversation. Claire and Hugh were sent off in the direction of Lady Ellis and her daughters, while the duchess fairly propelled herself in Sir Thomas's way. Miss Patterson herself took on Mrs. Thrasher, which Louisa thought was only natural considering that they knew one another. Trying to keep in touch with all that was going on was difficult since it remained necessary for her to keep time to the music. It was at about the moment that the protectors of Lady Landor met their adversaries that Louisa realized that the attention of that part of the company not engaged in dancing was concentrated on the drama which was unfolding on the sides.

Now it was time for Louisa and her partner to advance cross-handed down the line. When she next had pause enough to see what was happening, Miss Patterson was talking to Mrs. Thrasher with great intensity, and that stout personage was puffing in an indignant fashion. At the same time, the duchess had Sir Thomas by the arm and was leading him to a quiet corner, while, to Louisa's amazement, Hugh was making a great to-do with the three Miss Ellises who had clustered about him like great limpets clinging to a rock, leaving Claire and their mother to engage in a curiously friendly conversation.

The music finally ended, much to Louisa's relief, and she left her startled partner staring after her as she hurried across the floor to join Miss Patterson and her puffing companion.

"Dear Louisa," the headmistress cried with an archness which rang altogether false. "Mrs. Thrasher and I were having such a delightful exchange that I am glad you found it possible to join us. Only fancy! I just remembered such an amusing incident from the past."

"All that I can say is that your memory is deceiving you, Miss Patterson," the stout woman puffed indignantly. "I have been in Bath, of course. Everyone goes to take the waters at one time or another. Certainly I do not recollect anything so amusing as to make you smile in that particular manner."

"It will make such a delightful story," Miss Patterson continued with that same strange archness. "A dining-out story, I believe they're called."

Mrs. Thrasher was clearly angry. Indeed, she seemed to expand like a balloon. "A dining-out story, indeed," she thundered. "What do you know of dining-out, Miss Patterson? We may be distant cousins, but you know nothing of this world. This is *my* milieu, and I will not have you dining-out on stories about me."

"It is a great pity that you do not follow your own advice," Miss Patterson said quickly with her dark eyes sparkling in just the sort of way that Louisa had seen them do when some student was about to be severely dealt with. "Miss Rogers has told me enough to assure me that, far from being someone who would keep a watchful eye out for her, you are a vicious woman. Years ago when you came to visit my mother I knew that you were someone who devoured scandal, but then, many people do. I never thought, when I wrote you that letter, that you would take an active part in defaming the very lady Miss Rogers's father means to marry."

Mrs. Thrasher's eyes were so deeply sunk in flesh that it was difficult for them to narrow, but, in so far as it was possible, they did. "I cannot believe that you can condone the situation as it exists," she hissed. "The woman's morals are in shreds, and yet you allow this girl to remain in her house. Worse, you stay there, too. And now you dare to threaten me with . . ."

"I have threatened you with nothing worse than a story which will make you look even more ridiculous than you do already," Miss Patterson said quickly. "If you do not mind a few laughs at your expense—for you did look very funny in that public bath when the canvas cover-all that you were wearing . . ."

"Enough!" Mrs. Thrasher declared. "You have made your point for this evening. But I still believe that Captain Rogers should be told the truth about Lady Landor before it is too late."

And with that, she turned and huffed and puffed away. Neither she nor Miss Patterson had troubled to keep their voices down, and there were some interested spectators who drifted slowly away, ladies and gentlemen in all their finery, discussing the latest morsel with great relish.

"I am afraid that I allowed myself to be carried away," the headmistress said apologetically. "I should have insisted that she and I have our . . . discussion out in a more private place."

"Oh, you were fine," Louisa told her. "What a retreat you put her into. But I never would have thought you capable of blackmail! Did she really lose her canvas bathing cover?"

"I was standing with my mother by the window of the Pump Room which overlooks the King's Bath," Miss Patterson told her. "And Mrs. Thrasher was wallowing in the hot spring water along with a good many others. And then, quite suddenly . . ."

She covered her lips with her slender fingers, but she could not keep from laughing, and Louisa joined her, both of them convulsed by the thought of massive Mrs. Thrasher without her bathing costume. And it came to Louisa suddenly that her headmistress looked quite different than she had looked in the classroom. A few tendrils of black hair had come loose from the chignon and had fallen softly about her face. Her cheeks were flushed as well, and she looked anything but severe. Even if she had donned her gold-rimmed spectacles, Louisa thought that she would have looked almost beautiful. Indeed, as the musicians struck up a quadrille and Captain Rogers led Lady Landor to the dance floor, Louisa saw her father take a second glance at the headmistress in a way which seemed to indicate that he had not recognized her at first.

Three young gentlemen asked Louisa to dance, but she refused them all and hurried off to Claire who was standing alone in an alcove.

"How did you keep Lady Ellis quiet?" Louisa demanded. "What could you possibly have said to make her retire from the field?"

Instead of answering directly, Claire pointed her closed fan in the direction of the dance floor where Hugh was manipulating Miss Fanny Ellis about in time to the music with a look of patient suffering on his face. Miss Ellis, on the contrary, was smiling a smile so broad as to make her face seem to be composed of nothing but teeth jutting out in all directions. Her two sisters stood on the sidelines, bobbing up and down on their toes in an excited sort of way.

"They are waiting their turn," Claire said, smiling. "Poor Hugh. It was the ultimate sacrifice, but he has promised to dance with all of them. It was, I might add, his own idea."

"Were things so very desperate?" Louisa asked her. "Was she bent on doing damage?"

Claire pushed back a fair curl which had fallen on her forehead. "You should have heard her," she replied in the hushed tones of one who marvels at something they do not completely understand. "The malice simply ooozes out of her. She meant to tell your father a thing or two, she said. And she intended to do it in front of Lady Landor. Why, she went on and on about how Lady Landor had entrapped her brother. That seems to be her major grievance. She would also warn him that it was too late in life for him to marry."

Louisa's dark-fringed eyes sparkled excitedly. "I think I know why that woman is so vengeful," she exclaimed. "No doubt if her brother had died unmarried, the fortune would have been left to her. I do not know enough about their family matters to be certain, but I do know that Lady Landor was left everything. Where the title went, I am not sure. A nephew, perhaps. No matter. With only three daughters, Lady Ellis could have had no hopes of the title. But the money could have come to her if he had not married."

"How ugly motives often are," Claire said thoughtfully. "That is why Miles does not care overmuch for society. He says that no one can be trusted about anything except that they are certain to act in their own self-interest.''

''I did not know that he was such a cynic,'' Louisa retorted. ''But were he here tonight, we could prove him wrong. Certainly Hugh is not acting from self-interest now.''

Taking another look at his long-suffering expression, Claire agreed that that certainly was the case and promised to tell her brother about it when he returned.

''Not that anyone knows when that will be,'' she said. ''For that matter, no one ever knows where he has gone. But, if he wants to make a mystery of his goings, that is up to him. At least that is what Mama says. La! There is the Duchess. I saw her escorting Sir Thomas away from Lady Landor. How was it, I wonder, that she succeeded?''

But it seemed that the duchess was not ready to explain just how she had made such a great success. ''Sir Thomas is very conscious of his position in society,'' she told the two girls when they asked. ''My own position is unassailable and his is not. Still, even though he agreed not to make himself troublesome this evening, I do not think that anything I said will keep him from your father in the end, child.''

And she reached up to pat Louisa's curls, as though she were a child.

''I suppose,'' Claire said with some hesitation, ''it will not matter, if he loves her. I mean to say, surely he will not believe . . .''

She broke off as the duchess stiffened, and Louisa, looking over her shoulder, saw that, the gavotte just having ended, the Duke of Taxton had interrupted the captain and Lady Landor and was clearly making her an offer to next take to the dance floor with him.

''Why, he has not danced in donkey's years,'' Louisa heard the duchess mutter, and glancing back at her, she saw a curious look in the little woman's eyes. Could it be that she was jealous of the attentions which her husband was lavishing on Lady Landor? She would fight the impulse, of course, but she was only human, and the duke was clearly quite enthralled.

It was obvious that Lady Landor could not keep from flirting. Now she was taking the duke's arm and throwing back her turbaned head to laugh at some joke or other. Louisa saw her father looking after them, and the smile which had been on his face when he had given Lady Landor over the the duke was slowly fading.

And then the moment passed with the arrival of Miss Patterson beside him. The headmistress smiled and said a word. She looked out onto the dance floor, and somehow Louisa was certain that she was praising Lady Landor. It was so generous, so like her, that Louisa felt a little pang. And later, when a waltz had begun and she was sweeping around the floor in the arms of a handsome viscount, she saw that Miss Patterson and her father were dancing too. The headmistress's eyes were almost closed, as she swayed to the music, and Louisa, thinking of Miss Patterson storing up her memories, found herself wishing that the world had been fashioned in such a way that everyone, not just a few, could be happy.

Chapter Sixteen

THE next afternoon, at Miss Patterson's suggestion, the ladies attended a concert at Hervey Hall, just off the Strand. The performer was the contralto, Miss Irene Davis, whom, the headmistress assured them, it was a privilege to hear since she had chosen to retire long before it was time.

"Her last appearance was in Milan," the headmistress said to Lady Landor. "That was three years ago, I think. Perhaps you traveled over from Florence to hear her, as it was a rare occasion, I believe. I cannot think of the opera she performed in, but everyone who heard her then says that she was just reaching the top of her form."

Louisa was fond enough of music, but the thought of listening to another woman performing for an hour did not seem to spark any particular enthusiasm in Lady Landor, who declared that she had never seen the opera in Milan, with the air of one thankful for small favors. However, as it happened that Captain Rogers meant to spend the afternoon at his club, she agreed to accompany Louisa and Miss Patterson, and accordingly decked herself out to the nines in a stunning green chemise gown with a richly embroidered sabretache bag hung from a belt at the waist. Her bonnet was dashingly trimmed with ribbons, and altogether, she looked quite charming in a brilliant sort of way. Beside her Louisa, in pale blue muslin, looked delicate and lovely, while Miss Patterson, in prim and proper gray, might well have been setting out from her academy with two of her charges for a cultural excursion.

The contralto voice of Miss Davis rose and fell with skillful ease while Lady Landor looked around her, clearly thinking nothing of the music. Since the audience was composed almost entirely of ladies, she soon put an end to making small distractions such as beating out the rhythm with her fan on the edge of the seat and lapsed into a thoughtful state of such a great intensity that her lovely eyelids soon slid shut and the music became only an accompaniment to her dreams.

As for Louisa, she found her own attention wandering as she thought of the evening before at Almack's. In her fondest dreams she had never imagined that all three of Lady Landor's enemies could have been beaten into such a retreat. Indeed, had it not been for the undue attention Lady Landor had paid to the Duke of Taxton, she would have counted the evening as a great success. But it troubled her to remember the look in the duchess's eyes, a look which had soured as the evening had progressed. Louisa only hoped that, in the clear light of morning, the duchess would realize that Lady Landor could, apparently, no more refrain from flirting than from breathing.

It only troubled her that she could not be certain that Lady Landor's past was as innocent as she proclaimed. Certainly she, as her champion, should have a more total confidence that Lady Landor had stated the whole case to her. A lonely wife seeking English companionship in a foreign city was a natural thing. There was nothing wrong in her having spent her afternoons with English friends occasionally, if they had been ladies, as she claimed. Still, as the contralto's rich voice filled the hall, it came to Louisa that only a few details changed would make a world of difference in the truth of Lady Landor's past.

In times like these she found she often thought of Lord Cardross. It was a reassurance that he had chosen to think the best of the lady that her father meant to marry. Indeed, when he returned, he would try to muster proof that Sir Thomas Tigger maligned her in what he said. Claire had said her brother was a cynic. And Louisa trusted Claire. She was her friend. She saw her now nearly every day. If she called him cynic then that was what he was. Certainly he was a man of the world.

Why, Louisa wondered, did the thought of him make her so uncomfortable? Did it bother her that he had been witness to one of her failed attempts to thwart the enemy? Or was she bothered by his clear impression that she was reckless, that she had fallen in with the plans of Michelle Rioux and her brother quite so readily? But how had he known of that? She herself had never said a word. But he knew a great deal more than she. That much was clear. Just as he had predicted, she had not had even a glimpse of the brother and sister for the past few days. He had predicted they would disappear, and it appeared they had. At the same time he himself had had to go. Louisa wondered if there was a connection. And why did she feel this ache inside?

When the concert was over, they rode home in Lady Landor's open carriage, and it was only natural that they should go by way of The Mall. As before, heads turned and there were whispers. The few people who greeted them with bows and smiles were those who had attended the duchess's party. As for the remainder of the *haut ton*, nothing seemed to have changed at all. Lady Landor was still a curiosity, and it did not help matters particularly, from Louisa's point of view, that the young gentlemen whom she had danced with at the few entertainments she had gone to, made a great point of raising their hats to her exclusively.

Still, her mood was not too troubled when they reached the house on Grosvenor Square. But when they walked into the drawing room, pulling off bonnets and pelisses and listening to Lady Landor chatter, time came to a dramatic stop. For ever after Louisa was to remember her father as he stood there in the center of all that Oriental splendor, waiting for them in a clear state of great wrath.

"My dear!" Lady Landor exclaimed. "Whatever is the matter? Did you expect to find us here and were disappointed? Have you been waiting long? I declare, I never would have gone to that tiresome concert if I had known that you would be here. Come. Let me call for some claret to calm you. I cannot bear to see you in a temper."

And, with that, she pulled the bell rope with great vigor and hurried across the room to take her intended's arm. As for Louisa and Miss Patterson, they met one another's eye with the greatest trepidation, guessing that what they had most feared had happened.

"I—I encountered a gentleman at White's," the captain said stiffly, "who told me the most incredible stories."

A footman having entered the room in answer to the bell, he suspended further statements until the order for claret had been given.

"And perhaps some ratafia for us, as well," Lady Landor added. Then, when the footman had left the room: "But, my dear, London is full of incredible stories of all sorts. You should know that better than I, it seems. Why is it that you should be so concerned?''

Handsome though he still was, Louisa had never seen certain lines on his face before. They aged him, and she felt a great surge of resentment that this had happened to disturb his happiness.

''I am concerned,'' he said turning to Lady Landor, ''because the stories concerned you, my dear. I thought at first that I should say nothing to you of the matter. But it does not matter. Sooner or later you would have heard, at any rate.''

''Heard what?'' Lady Landor demanded. ''Stories concerning me? Stories to disturb you? Why, I can hardly credit it.''

''Perhaps,'' Louisa heard Miss Patterson say in a voice best noted for its calm, ''it would be best if we first knew who told you these stories, sir. They might not be worth repeating.''

''Yes, father,'' Louisa chorused. ''If the gentleman cannot be credited, there is no reason that you should give the details.''

Captain Rogers looked at his daughter with rising comprehension. ''You are not surprised,'' he said in amazement. ''Neither are you, Miss Patterson. Why, both of you have been privy to these reports before me, haven't you?''

''How can we be certain until you tell us who told them to you, sir,'' Miss Patterson said with quiet dignity. ''If you are about to mention the name of Sir Thomas Tigger, I believe that it is quite true that we know what you are speaking of.''

Louisa noted that Lady Landor turned a trifle pale at the mention of Sir Thomas's name. But by the time the footman had made another interruption and had served claret to the captain and the ladies, she had quite regained her composure, as though this was nothing more than she had expected.

''It *was* Sir Thomas,'' Captain Rogers said grimly, drinking his claret at a single quaff. ''I do not know the gentleman, but he made a point of seeking an introduction to me and proceeded to . . .''

''Did he malign me?'' Lady Landor said quite coolly. ''For if he did then you should know the reason. In Florence, where he was now and then part of the English community, he made himself a nuisance, if you understand me. Every time we met he would profess the greatest admiration. And I made every effort to avoid him but . . .''

"What is this?" the captain demanded, setting down his glass. "The English community, indeed. You gave me to understand, I think, that you remained by your husband's side entirely while you were in Florence. And he could abide no one English with him except you, my dear."

"Why, there has been some misunderstanding," Lady Landor told him with a coquettish smile. "I never meant to make you think my husband kept me prisoner. I was allowed to join English companions for afternoon rides and promenades. I assure you, my dear Robert, that I would have gone quite insane had it been otherwise. It was on these occasions, over the years, that I now and then met Sir Thomas—even though I avoided those opportunities, once I determined that he was a danger. But he is a hateful and persistant man. Once I rejected his advances entirely, he became petulant and then revengeful. I do not know what he has been saying about me, but you can count on it that nothing which he has reported is true."

Louisa could not help but admire her bravado. Still, why did that particular word spring to mind? Her response might just as well be that of a complete innocent, someone so far distanced from guile that there was no difficulty in presenting her case clearly.

"You do not have to defend yourself to me, my darling," the captain told her. "I should have guessed his motives were something of the sort. I did not doubt you for an instant, although I did think it odd . . . But no matter! The fellow will pay for the scandal he has been spreading, for I have called him out."

The moment that he said it, everything seemed to freeze in place. Lady Landor stood with her hands pressed to her lips. Miss Patterson, who had sunk down on a chair, kept her dark eyes on Captain Rogers's face. As for Louisa, she felt the shock so severely that for a moment she felt faint.

"You must not do it!" Lady Landor cried, breaking the silence with a voice gone shrill and high. "I will not let you fight a duel. Not a duel over my reputation. There is no need to do it. Let the scoundrel tell his stories. No one will believe him anyway. No one could possibly . . ."

Her voice trailed off, and Louisa saw the dawning recognition on her face, a face which, for a moment, fell into haggard lines. One could see what she would look like when her age asserted itself, as someday it must. The lush beauty crushed was like a crumpled rose which could do nothing but languish.

"Oh no," she cried, turning to Miss Patterson and Louisa. "That was why they greeted us with silence at Almack's—that first time and last night. That was why there have been no invitations, or rather, only two. That is why, when I go riding in the park, some ladies look the other way when I go past. Oh dear, I cannot bear it. To think that they should have heard such stories . . ."

It came to Louisa to wonder how it was that Lady Landor seemed to be referring to the stories as though she knew their content. And then she thought it only natural that the older woman would guess the sort of thing that a gentleman scorned, as Sir Thomas Tigger had been, would say.

"My dear . . ." the captain said, but Lady Landor hurried to the door, her face hidden in her hands. It was as though she knew what had happened to her beauty and did not want it to show.

"Let me come with you," the captain said, following her. "There is no need for fear, I tell you. We are to use pistols, and I am an excellent shot. Furthermore, I do not mean to kill the blackguard, but rather wound him in the shoulder of the hand which holds the gun. You will be vindicated, my dear, and Tigger will have been punished. There is no other way for it to go."

"No, no!" Lady Landor cried as he tried to pull her hands away from her face. "I cannot let you do it, Robert. I will find some way to prevent it. For the present, let me go. Maria will take care of me. I want no one but Maria to be with me now."

"I think she means it," Miss Patterson said, rising to put out a restraining hand as the captain made as though he meant to follow her. "Sometimes women are better for being left along."

"Yes, yes," Captain Rogers said absently. "No doubt you are right."

"Papa!" Louisa cried, going to put her arms around him. "Are you certain that you must do this?"

They looked at one another, the young beauty with her tangled curls and the grizzled-haired gentleman in his blue jacket which gave no hint of the military.

"Quite certain," he said at last, kissing her forehead. "But you are not to worry."

"The fact is, sir," Miss Patterson interrupted in her even voice, "that there is always need for worry when two men duel. There is too much room for chance. Furthermore, I think that if this becomes common knowledge—and what use is it if it does not—it will only serve to bring you the disapproval of the army and perhaps of the Prince Regent himself."

The captain's handsome face was drawn into grim lines. As had been the case with Lady Landor, suddenly he looked his age. Louisa found herself hating the circumstances which had created this metamorphosis. Suddenly she did not care whether Lady Landor was innocent or not. If it had not been for her, her father would never have been put in this fresh danger.

"And there is this," she said impulsively, prepared to add the only argument she could to the case Miss Patterson had made, "what if it happens, after all is said and done, that . . ."

The headmistress must have guessed what she was about to say, must have guessed that Louisa meant to remind her father that the stories that Sir Thomas Tigger were spreading might be true. Catching the girl's arm, she squeezed it tight by way of warning.

"What your daughter means is that the duel may show nothing except your confidence that the lady you mean to marry is innocent," she said.

"Quite so," the captain told her. "That may be all that comes of it. But the world will know that I am certain of her innocence. It is a gesture. Nothing more. But it is a gesture I must make."

Chapter Seventeen

NEITHER Louisa nor Miss Patterson tried to keep him from leaving. It was clear to both of them that he needed to be alone. They stood arm in arm by the long window which faced east and watched him stride off down the street with his shoulders set in just such a manner as to indicate the degree of tension inside him.

"We must find some way to prevent this," Louisa said in a low voice when he had turned the corner and was out of sight. "From what I have seen of Sir Thomas, I would not think him an expert marksman, but you were quite right when you said that in dueling there is too much room for chance. Besides, no matter how much I despise the gentleman, I do not want my father to take the chance of killing him. Lady Landor's morality may be a serious matter, but it does not call, I think, for the spilling of a single drop of blood."

"It is only natural that you should be somewhat bitter," the headmistress told her. "If she had been a different sort of woman, no one would have believed the rumors about her. But, particularly now, you must hide your feelings from your father. No doubt he feels protective of her to a great degree."

Louisa pressed her headmistress's arm gratefully. "I have been struggling with certain feelings against her ever since Papa mentioned the duel," she confessed. "How clever you are to guess what I had been thinking. But I am afraid that I have gone even further than you guessed. I have entertained such notions . . ."

"You wonder if she may, indeed, be innocent," Miss Patterson said for her. "That, too, is only to be expected. Her behavior with the Duke of Taxton the other evening was thoughtless, at the least. She should have seen that the duchess was annoyed, but she seems never to think of consequences. She has a child's air of reckless abandon often. Witness her emotional reaction to your father's news. No doubt even in Florence, there were times when she, uncalculatingly, made errors. We must consider that to be a distinct possibility.''

Louisa looked out the window at the quiet square. A young girl and a gentleman walked together on the further verge, and she could see her laughing up at him, see the happy smile under the deep rim of the bonnet. How good it would be, she thought, to be that carefree. It came to Louisa that, with Lady Landor as her stepmother, there were apt to be a good many awkward moments, a great deal of holding in of breath. And, of course, if she did not want to place a strain on her relations with her father, she must always pretend not to mind. For the first time she clearly faced the consequences of the marriage and felt a sense of falling inside, as though she was about to lose something very important to her, although precisely what that was she could not be sure.

''I must trust my father absolutely,'' Louisa murmured.

''Never trust anyone that far, my child,'' Miss Patterson said gently. She had apparently forgotten to put on her gold-rimmed spectacles for the occasion of the concert, and there was something looser about her hair. Whatever the reason, Louisa was not as much reminded of the classroom as she had expected to be whenever the headmistress gave advice.

''But, in this case, what can I do?'' the girl demanded. ''I can argue with him against the duel. But if he would not listen to Lady Landor when she made such an emotional appeal, why should he listen to me? And if he means to marry her, as he clearly does, I must have no doubts about her, or I will risk losing him.''

Miss Patterson arched her fingers together and pressed them against her upper lip in a way she had of doing when she was thoughtful.

''I think that we must try to determine precisely whom your father plans to defend with his very life,'' she said. ''Clearly we cannot listen to Sir Thomas or Lady Ellis or Mrs. Thrasher. But there must be someone in London who knew or heard of Lady Landor in Florence and can vouch for her reputation.''

Louisa ran one hand through her tangled curls and shrugged her shoulders wearily. ''That was what Lord Cardross intended to do,'' she said, turning away from the window and dropping into a wing chair. ''He said that we ought to know the truth, whatever it may be, and I see now how right he was.''

''Then let us take some action,'' Miss Patterson urged. ''If we can get the necessary evidence, there will be no need for a duel.

Once Sir Thomas is publicly proven a liar, he will be beneath your father's notice.''

Louisa closed her eyes, and the thick fringe of her lashes curled on her ivory skin. "I do not know where to start," she said quite simply. "If only Lord Cardross were here."

Just at that moment, the door was opened and the footman declared that a gentleman had come to wait on Miss Rogers. "It is Lord Cardross, miss," he said. "Will you receive him?"

"Only have him wait a minute," Louisa exclaimed in great excitement, starting from the chair. "Or perhaps five. Take him to the blue salon, Andrews. Tell him that Miss Patterson and I will join him there as promptly as possible."

When the footman had left the room, Louisa saw that she was being observed narrowly. "How does it happen that you did not simply have him ushered in?" the headmistress observed. "After all, it was as though you were a genie rubbing a lantern. You wished him here and he appeared. I would have expected you to welcome him with open arms."

Louisa tried her best to keep from blushing, but it was too late. She could not even manage to turn before she had been observed.

"I did not mean that in the literal sense," Miss Patterson said dryly. "My dear, you give yourself away no matter in which direction you look. Lord Cardross means a great deal to you, does he not?"

"Indeed, he is no more than a friend," Louisa protested. "Pray never insinuate anything to the contrary, even to me. Why, the gentleman would be horrified if he thought that I considered him in a romantic manner. He has been kind and patient, and he has seen me as the ninny that I am . . .''

Miss Patterson smiled patiently. "A ninny, are you?" she demanded. "Nothing could be further from the truth, my dear. That, at least, I can assure you. But then you know my regard for your intelligence."

"But I acted like a fool when I first came to London!" Louisa cried, finding that she could do nothing to keep the story from pouring out of her. "I was so completely confident, you see. Mrs. Thrasher told me about the rumors, and I snubbed her. Turned and left her in the park. As though my incivility could mean anything one way or the other."

"You are too hard on yourself, my dear Louisa."

"On the contrary, it has been all too clear to me that I am a perfect innocent. When I went to interview Lady Ellis, I accomplished nothing. By the time I set out to deal with Sir Thomas Tigger, Lord Cardross felt sorry enough for me to lend a hand. And he consequently was witness to my humiliation."

Miss Patterson, cool and unruffled in her plain gray gown and loosely knotted hair, folded her hands in front of her, as though she meant to set an example of calmness which Louisa would do well to emulate.

"I am certain that you exaggerate, my dear," she said. "Only remember what a success we were last evening."

"And what a failure all our efforts have come to today," Louisa reminded her. "We only put off the evil moment. The Duchess was able to persuade Sir Thomas to stay quiet for the evening, but he was out and about early enough today. If Lord Cardross has not heard of the duel, we must tell him. La, I cannot think why he has come here unless it is to tell me that he intends to continue the search for someone to vouch for Lady Landor."

"If you keep him waiting longer, he will think you do not care," Miss Patterson suggested. "Here. Let me just smooth your hair. Would you prefer to be alone with him? I mean to say, since there is no romantic involvement, it could easily be allowed."

"Do not leave!" Louisa exclaimed. "I—I want your company during our interview. Perhaps you can come up with some idea . . . And then we must tell him about my father. Oh, dear. Why must I behave like a perfect fool?"

"You are behaving like an enamored young lady," the headmistress told her dryly, "even though I know that is not true. Come, let us go down the hall together. And stop our chatter. Let Lord Cardross see us in a thoughtful mood which suits the moment."

Miss Patterson opened the door to the blue salon, and Louisa saw him, standing by the fireplace, tall and more handsome than she had remembered him in his blue jacket and buckskin breeches, covered to the knees with glistening Hessian boots. His dark hair was as carelessly arranged as usual, and the look he directed at them was intense.

"I am sorry to keep you waiting, sir," Louisa began.

But before she could go on, he had bowed to her and to Miss Patterson and gone directly to the point.

"On my return to London," he said, "I went to White's, Miss Rogers, intending to meet your father. There was a certain business for us to transact. But I was told that he had left the club in a fury, and that he had challenged Sir Thomas Tigger to a duel. I came directly here to discover if that information was true."

He was nothing if not businesslike, Louisa thought, hoping, at the same time, that this would show Miss Patterson that there was, indeed, nothing between them. To heighten the effect, she answered in the same crisp tone.

"My father has just left us, sir," she said. "And there has been such a challenge. You will not be surprised to discover that I do not know what to do."

"We had thought to find some evidence which would make such an encounter needless, sir," Miss Patterson said in her low, even voice. "Any suggestions that you could make would be appreciated, as you must assume. But you must make them to Miss Rogers, I fear, since I have certain duties . . ."

And, with that, she drifted from the room before Louisa could stop her. The girl felt her face flame and kept her back to the visitor, in the position she had assumed when the headmistress had left them.

He cleared his throat. Louisa knew that she must turn and face him, only hoping, as she did so, that he would not notice her discomposure. How unkind Miss Patterson had been, she told herself. No doubt she had thought of matchmaking, which only showed that she did not understand the situation.

"Miss Rogers," Lord Cardross began, "I have known your father for a long time, and I regard him as someone I would make every effort to oblige. But I find myself in a difficult situation."

Louisa forced herself to raise her thick-fringed eyes to his. "And what would that be, sir?" she inquired. "I know that you have been out of London, and perhaps you have not be informed . . ."

"I know that you and others made a valiant effort last evening to keep your father and his intended from embarrassment," he said in a low voice, his eyes never once leaving her face. "And I know you were successful. But I am certain that you must have realized that Sir Thomas Tigger could not be prevented from making his case to him. Which is what happened today at White's, as far as I can discover."

"My father is beside himself with outrage," Louisa told him. "Lady Landor has begged him not to defend her, but nothing she or anyone could say will carry any weight with him. Of that I am quite sure."

To her surprise, Lord Cardross came toward her and took her by the hand. "Come and sit down, Miss Rogers," he said in a voice full of concern. "All of this has been difficult for you, I understand."

"I am quite prepared to cope, sir," Louisa retorted, resisting his invitation for her to take a chair. "If only someone could be found who knew Lady Landor in Florence. Someone other than Sir Thomas, I mean. Some person who could vouch for her good character. . . ."

"I have been in contact with someone who knew of her when she was abroad," Lord Cardross interrupted. "And I am afraid that, although Sir Thomas's slander has not be substantiated, Lady Landor did not always behave with the greatest propriety. There is enough in it to make it ill-advised to call Sir Thomas out for lying. I had hoped to contact your father before that became the case. You will remember perhaps, Miss Rogers, that this is more or less what I predicted."

She could not take it in so suddenly. "Then do you mean that she behaved in—in an immoral way?" she asked him, this time needing no offer from him as an excuse to sink onto a chair.

Lord Cardross shook his head, but his expression remained grim. "The word does not suit you, Miss Rogers," he said. "What would you know of immorality?"

"I have read widely!" she told him. And then, too late, realized how absurd that would, no doubt, sound.

"Yes, there is that," he said, without a smile. "I did not mean to mock you. No, she was not immoral in the technical sense. But she was frivolous beyond belief, given her position. And she encouraged gentlemen—among them, apparently, Sir Thomas. No doubt she acted innocently . . ."

"Flirtation is as natural to her as breathing," Louisa told him. "I am certain that she would not, intentionally, have done anything wrong."

"I hope that you are right," he said in a low voice, standing over her, looking down with those disturbing dark eyes. "But the truth of it is that your father may put himself in danger for a cause—forgive me—that is not completely worthy."

For a moment there was silence between them. "Is that what you intend to tell my father?" Louisa demanded finally.

"If there is anything to tell him," Lord Cardross replied, "surely Lady Landor should be the one to tell him. The duel is to be held at the western edge of Hyde Park, I understand. The location is supposed to be a secret, but I found someone . . . No matter. Will you do your best to persuade Lady Landor to be honest with your father, Miss Rogers. If you succeed, someone's life can certainly be saved."

Chapter Eighteen

"First of all, I think we should all be seen in public together," Louisa said. "That will assure everyone that Papa takes no stock of the rumors Sir Thomas has been spreading."

"But what about tomorrow?" Miss Patterson said. "What you propose will do nothing to change the plans made for a duel."

"Something may happen in the meantime," Lord Cardross said in a low voice. "In my opinion, Miss Rogers's idea is a good one. Allow me to suggest the time and place. Given that it must be this evening, I think an appearance at Vauxhall Gardens might be in order. A special fireworks display is planned, and nearly all of the *haut ton* will be in attendance."

"You understand what I have in mind then," Louisa said eagerly. "I mean to show my father that if, by appearing together, we make it clear that he has taken no notice of Sir Thomas's accusations, there may be no need for a duel. Papa will see it, I am sure."

"I cannot think it can all be solved so easily," Lady Landor said in a puzzled voice, "but I will do whatever you resolve."

It was later that same afternoon. Louisa had taken Lord Cardross's comments seriously. She would do everything she could to keep her father from a duel with Sir Thomas. And she would try to protect Lady Landor's reputation, even though, from what Lord Cardross had told her, it might well be a losing cause.

Miss Patterson had been the one responsible for bringing Lady Landor downstairs again. Having found her indulging in hysterics with Maria in attendance in her bedchamber, the headmistress had managed to convince her that it was her responsibility to put her emotions in the background until the captain's problem could be resolved.

"She had taken recourse to a dose of laudanum before I reached her," the headmistress had warned Louisa and Lord Cardross when she had rejoined them in the blue salon. "That has made her calmer and then, too, I am afraid I was severe. But I have so little patience with ladies who indulge themselves in emotional displays. . . . Still, I expect no one should blame her."

When Lady Landor had joined them, she had been so much subdued that she had taken Louisa by surprise. No doubt it was the laudanum which had changed her so abruptly into someone so disheartened, and it occurred to the girl that, no matter what happened, she did not want this ebullient lady to be changed by her experiences. Flirt she might be. Perhaps, even worse. But she was charming in her own flamboyant way, and when changed, as now, the beauty somehow departed from the chestnut hair and ivory skin. The brown eyes, no longer liquid, were lackluster. Louisa could not help but feel sorry for her as she saw her take her seat on the settee and fold her hands. She was, Louisa noticed, wearing her "sad" dress as it should be worn, without a flare.

"But how will we persuade Papa to go on an outing?" Louisa demanded. "He was in no mood to look at fireworks when he left here."

"More in a mood to make them himself," Miss Patterson said absently. "But, yes, that is a problem."

"La," Lady Landor said wearily. "I can very well persuade him if I care to make the effort. I know all the ways."

And that, Louisa thought with sudden inspiration, was the saddest thing about the lady. From the moment her duke had claimed her, from the minute that her father had given him her hand, she had been expected to do nothing more than ornament her husband's household, to be a charming decoration. And, no doubt, she had soon learned all the pretty ways with which she could get her own way, since she could not exist completely without power. And, yes, no doubt, she could twist her captain about her finger in any matter which was not vital. Distraught as he was and angry, he would not be able to refuse her the chance to see some fireworks.

The crushing thing was that Lady Landor must also know the extent of her influence. Louisa noticed that she had not offered to dissuade him from fighting duels. Over the years, no doubt, she had tested how far she could go and discovered the exact proportion of the prizes she could demand and win. But perhaps, the girl told herself, this was all that Lady Landor had ever wanted. And that was even sadder still.

Suddenly she knew that her father must not marry this woman. Whether she had compromised herself in the past was beside the point. Even with a pristine pure reputation, she would only bore the captain in time. No doubt her beauty had beguiled him. Perhaps her innocent extravagance had its appeal. But in time she would come to bore him, no matter how often and how long his military duties called him away. Furthermore, whenever he left her behind him, she would go on her merry way in a fashion which would make her a constant prey of rumor, whether or not she did anything really wrong. Sir Thomas would not be the only gentleman the captain would be called on to fight a duel with.

Could she make him see it, Louisa wondered. Certainly it was nothing she could tell him, not unless she dared to risk a lasting anger which might change everything between thm. She started as she became aware that Lord Cardross was speaking.

"Perhaps I can convince him," he told them. "No doubt he will have gone back to his rooms . . ."

"Sir Thomas Tigger!" Lady Landor said suddenly in a loud voice which blurred but still contained considerable disdain. "He is a French sympathizer, you know."

Louisa could see from the dazed expression of the lady's eyes that the laudanum was having its effect. She wondered if Lady Landor knew what she was saying or if she should be taken seriously.

"What an odd thing to say," Miss Patterson murmured. "I wonder if she really means it?"

"He is not a pleasant person," Lord Cardross said, turning his dark eyes on Lady Landor, "But to go so far as to say that he supports Napoleon . . ."

He was warning her not to continue. Suddenly Louisa was certain of it.

"I kept a close eye on him in Florence," Lady Landor said drowsily. "Just as close an eye on him as he had on me. Even, sometimes, in the evening . . ."

She paused and tried a little laugh which did not quite succeed. Louisa wondered if she was alert enough to know precisely what she had said. Presumably her only contact with the English community in Florence had been during the afternoons. Clearly, just as Lord Cardross had hinted to her, there was more to the story than Lady Landor had told her.

"I can list the names of all those people he has talked to during the past two years," Lady Landor continued. "Sir Thomas calls himself a traveler, and perhaps he is, but I do not think scandal is the only thing he reports. Indeed . . ."

But by now the drug was really taking its effect. Her voice became so listless that it could not proceed. Leaning her head against the chair, she fell into a sleep so profound that, later, when one of the footmen carried her up the stairs, she did not waken.

When she did come to herself, some hours later, Lady Landor said nothing of the charge she had made against Sir Thomas, and Louisa and Miss Patterson were of the opinion that she had forgotten what she had said when the drug had muddled her thinking. Besides, the thing now was to concentrate on the evening ahead, although Lord Cardross had been so withdrawn and thoughtful when he had left the house that the headmistress had seen fit to remind him and set the time.

The only difficulty which remained was created by Lady Landor who, although quite herself again in every way, took it into her head that under the circumstances she should dress in the most retiring sort of way. Indeed, she went so far as to ask Miss Patterson if she could borrow one of her dresses which made both Louisa and the headmistress laugh.

"The difference in size alone makes that impossible," Miss Patterson said gently. "You are built on classic lines, Lady Landor, and I have not been gifted in a like manner, as you see. Besides, you do not want to show that anything has changed for you or for the captain. That is the whole purpose of our making a show this evening. People must understand that Captain Rogers, having heard the worst, has not changed his attitude toward you one single jot. Certainly, nothing that Sir Thomas has to say should make you change your ways."

Louisa was relieved when Lady Landor gave way easily. As for her own feelings, they were extremely mixed. On the one hand, she could only hope that her father would see that this marriage should not be, before it was too late. And on the other, she felt guilty in encouraging Lady Landor to wear the blue silk dress which was so very fashionable as to be certain to cause comment. Had it not been for Miss Patterson's calming presence, she might well have felt quite hopeless about the situation. Lord Cardross had said that something must be done to prevent the duel. And she had proposed an outing. That did seem very little in the way of a possible solution. Oddly, he had seemed quite satisfied, and somehow Louisa felt certain that the young viscount had something on his mind, something she did not even guess at.

Louisa's first glimpse of Vauxhall, however, drove everything else out of her mind, at least for the moment. The lights that were strung between the trees threw their reflections on the surface of the river which bordered the pleasure garden. A great circular building with Greek and Roman touches in its construction provided alcoves which opened outward where there were tables at which wines and delicacies of every sort could be served. At the second level there was a platform where musicians were playing, filling the night with music. And all about there were walks lined with shrubs where people were walking.

"There are more of the hoi polloi here now than there were in my day," Lady Cardross said somewhat stiffly when they were settled at one of the tables which lined the pavilion and wine had been ordered. "I have heard that it has become a rather rowdy spot on occasion and that pickpockets are everywhere."

"Still, as Miles said, most of the *haut ton* will put in an appearance tonight," Claire reminded her, her pretty face half hidden by her bonnet, "because of the fireworks, which promise to be spectacular."

"We are attracting enough attention to satisfy your purposes, my dear," the Duchess of Taxton said to Louisa. "Everyone will know that your father has not been influenced by what Sir Thomas said."

And, indeed, Captain Rogers had satisfied all the requirements. Louisa did not know what Lord Cardross had said to him, but he looked quite different than he had looked this afternoon. Either the shock of what had happened had worn off, or he possessed some new information which had had a salutary effect. Furthermore, this evening, for some reason, he was wearing his officer's uniform with its red coat, as though he wanted to remind everyone who saw him that he was a member of the military. Louisa had the feeling that something very odd was going on, although she could not put her finger on it.

As for Lady Landor, she was a sight to be seen, for she had allowed her rich chestnut hair to tumble on her bare shoulders, covering the curls with a variety of glistening ornaments which made her hair look as though it were full of stars. Needless to say, without Miss Patterson's restraint, she had reverted to old habits and worn her bodice low. Earlier, as they had entered the garden side by side, Louisa had been more aware than ever of the contrast between them, with Lady Landor drenched in satin and herself slim in the girlish white muslin which was so often her choice, although she too had somewhat defied convention in wearing a primrose silk bandeau about her curls instead of donning a bonnet.

"I can remember being brought here when I was just a girl," Lady Landor said, swinging her white ivory fan back and forth before her lovely face. "I thought it was a fairyland then, and I see now that I was not mistaken."

"That is because you are a child, still, my dear," the Duke of Taxton told her, leaning forward to pour her a bit more wine. Louisa felt a twinge of impatience with the portly gentleman for showing so clearly that he thought Lady Landor so delightful. Surely he must be aware that when he said the sort of thing he had just now, the duchess would fall to frowning. And if he was too great a fool to notice, Lady Landor might make better observations. And yet she was looking at him now as though he were the most charming gentleman she had ever known before, and gently tapping his hand with her ivory fan.

"What a delight you are, sir," she teased him. "Always ready to compliment me in unusual ways. A child indeed! I hardly think so. Robert, do you not agree?"

But Captain Rogers was watching for something, Louisa saw, and she thought that Lord Cardross was doing the same. Certainly both of them seemed distracted, and their eyes were often to be found sorting through the shifting crowd.

"*I* will agree with the Duke, madam," Hugh Trever exclaimed. "You are childlike in the most graceful sort of way. I do not blame Captain Rogers for calling Sir Thomas out. If I were in his place, I would do the same."

Louisa bit her lip as she saw Claire begin to drum the table impatiently. Although, indeed, she did not know that she could blame her friend on the condition that ever since this evening had begun, Lady Landor had seemed to do her best to charm him. Strangely enough, all this did not seem to trouble the captain who remained distracted, his dark eyes searching the crowd.

The music being played above them came to a sudden stop at the same moment that a group of smartly dressed people appeared on one of the gravel walks. Louisa nearly started from her chair when she saw Michelle Rioux and her brother walking one on either side of Sir Thomas Tigger, who was talking for all that he was worth. Michelle, in an elegant poke bonnet, bent forward to hear him, while Claude assumed a watchful expression. Behind them came Lady Ellis and her daughters and Mrs. Thrasher, plump and puffing as usual, no doubt hungry for information about the duel and hoping to overhear some on-dit or other.

As Mademoiselle Rioux came abreast of Captain Rogers, she gave him a penetrating glance. Instantly the captain rose. Lord Cardross did the same. Mrs. Thrasher saw them first and pointed. Lady Ellis appeared to fall into a swoon and was supported by her daughters, each of whom looked distracted in her own distinctive way. As for Sir Thomas, he stopped dead in his tracks, a perfect fop, as always, with every stitch of his clothing as embroidered as there was room to be. "Well, gentlemen," he said quite coolly.

"Well, indeed," Lord Cardross said in a dry voice. As for Captain Rogers, he simply pointed at Sir Thomas, whereupon a military guard appeared from nowhere, two men in uniform, with muskets in their hands. While Sir Thomas looked about himself in horror, they came to stand on either side of him, as his companions fell back in consternation.

"We have only been waiting to accumulate enough evidence against you," Captain Rogers said. "You have been spying for the French, sir. At least that is the charge. Lady Landor will be among those giving evidence against you. May I say it is no more than you deserve."

Chapter Nineteen

"I see the fireworks do not amuse you, Miss Rogers," Lord Cardross said.

It was nearly midnight, and the sky above the river that twisted its way through London was alive with shining colors as rocket after rocket burst into the air. Below, the gardens of Vauxhall were full of people looking upward, and with each rocket's burst they cried out like the delighted children which, for a time at least, they were.

"After what has happened here this evening, I do not find it as easy as you to be distracted by some explosions in the sky, sir," Louisa told him. "But then, of course, you knew about this all along. At least that is my impression although, no doubt, it is all much too secret for you to talk about."

She was angry, and she could not hide it. For years she had accepted the fact that her father often went about secret business. She was accustomed to his sudden disappearances, to the fact that often he could not tell her where he was going. Ever since Napoleon had become the enemy of the English, she had guessed that her father's business, which often took him to the Continent, must have something to do with the French. But that had been when she was at school. It had not touched her, really, except to cause her to worry about whether he was safe. But now everything was different.

Earlier that evening, she had tried to explain the violence of her feelings to Miss Patterson. It had been directly after Sir Thomas had been taken away and libations were being drunk to a delighted Lady Landor, with even Claire and the duchess mellowed toward her now that she had become the toast of the evening.

"I cannot sit there and watch them," Louisa had said under her breath after she and the headmistress had excused themselves from the table with the excuse that they wanted to walk about a bit. "Not until this is all explained."

"Your father seems to have told you as much as he feels he can," Miss Patterson had said mildly. "Secrets were reaching Paris. Bits of information concerning the affairs of this country which were being picked up all about the Continent. On one of his last missions, your father came upon some information which pointed in Sir Thomas's way. And then, when it was discovered that Lady Landor could provide some substantiation, at least for Sir Thomas's activities in Florence . . ."

"How did my father come to know that?" Louisa had demanded as they had paced along the gravel path. "Indeed, I do not think she ever would have mentioned it had the laudanum not confused her. I will say this, she never carps against anyone, no matter how they have treated her. But this afternoon it did come out. And my father was not in attendance. Neither you nor I had opportunity to see him. Besides, I did not take what she said seriously, nor, I think, did you."

"That is true," Miss Patterson had told her thoughtfully. "I took it as a bit of delirium caused by the drug. "But Lord Cardross . . ."

"He took her seriously enough," Louisa replied. "I remember now the way he started. He must have gone directly to my father and reported. He, too, makes secret trips, you know. Claire says that there is no accounting for his comings and his goings. Do you not think that strange?"

"Do you mean you think that he goes on secret missions, like your father?" Miss Patterson had said. The revelation of Sir Thomas's perfidy had sobered her so much that she had taken her gold-rimmed spectacles from her reticule and put them on. "But, my dear child, he is not even in the army."

"How can we be certain?" Louisa demanded. "What do we really know about him? Only one thing, as far as I am concerned. And that is that he used us for his own purposes! There is scheming in this. We are only one part of a complicated puzzle that, it appears, is not to be explained."

All her anger had welled up when she had said that, and she had turned to the headmistress, her cheeks flushed and her blue eyes sparkling. The white cashmere shawl that she wore about her shoulders as protection against the night air slipped to the path and she did not notice.

"Only think of the facts," she told her companion. "Lady Landor came to London to be ignored, but only because Lord Cardross was out of town. The minute that he returned to the city from one of his mysterious missions, his mother presented an invitation, no doubt at his request. Was it because he knew that Lady Landor had information which she could give against Sir Thomas Tigger, or was it because he is my father's friend? Even that is not to be explained to us! One thing is certain. Lord Cardross's kind attempts to help me instate Lady Landor in society were not as disinterested as I supposed. I mean to say . . ."

Miss Patterson had picked up the shawl, and now she wrapped it tenderly around the slim shoulders. "I know what you mean to say," she had said in a whisper. "I have often known the feeling, my dear. But gentlemen *do* run the world. There is no question of it. Oh, I have fashioned my own little world. At the academy I am in charge and no one else. And it has struck me, as it has you—particularly tonight—that we are treated, we ladies, with extraordinary dispatch."

"Yes!" Louisa had said eagerly. "That is what I mean exactly. Claire and Lady Cardross and the others do not seem to mind. Sir Thomas is charged with treason before their very eyes and taken away. Lady Landor is proclaimed a heroine. She smiles and takes it as her due without a single question asked. And the others are content to toast her and celebrate and never have it explained precisely what happened."

Back at the pavilion, a group of ladies on the balcony were singing madrigals. It was a pleasant sound, but for Louisa the evening was spoiled.

"Ever since I came to London," she told the headmistress, "I knew that something was wrong. I mean to say, you gave me a fine education. And, like you, while I was at the academy, I felt the mistress of my little world. But once I reached the city and discovered how closely one must conform to the customs at the risk of being excluded . . . Oh, I am not putting this well at all! I mean to say, it *is* a narrow world, and I am expected to live my life in it. To laugh and smile and chatter mindlessly while all about me gentlemen go about their business and pause, occasionally, to pay me and all the other ladies a little condescending attention."

It had been such an outburst that she had finished it on the verge of tears. But weeping was one of the many things she *would* not do. Now, as the fireworks split against the sky, she decided that she would not stay silent, either. Lord Cardross had asked her what was wrong, and she meant to tell him.

"Momentous events occurred this evening," she said, turning her thick-fringed eyes on him. "And to my knowledge, no explanations have been made. We are expected to sit back and toast Lady Landor and watch the firecrackers and later say, 'Oh, my. How exciting.' And take it for granted that this is the best of all possible worlds where everything works out precisely as you gentlemen would have it. And explanations are offered or not, as you see fit."

There was a strange expression in Lord Cardross's dark eyes. A rocket exploding red and gold overhead made everyone about them exclaim. But they stood alone in their private circle of apartness, a circle which Louisa, in her anger, was only vaguely conscious of.

"Is your anger directed at me, Miss Rogers," Lord Cardross replied. "Or are you attacking the world in general? I might be able to defend myself, but I do not think I can defend the other."

The coolness of his irony offended Louisa. Did he think that she could be so easily turned away from questioning what had happened—really happened—here tonight?

She would have railed at him. Indeed, she had turned in his direction completely, her hands clenched in the folds of her cashmere shawl, when they were interrupted.

"My dear Miss Rogers," Lady Ellis said in a voice which was smooth as syrup, "I wanted you to know directly how much I regret having been taken in by that frightful creature. My daughters feel the same."

At this, Patience squinted up her eye, Fanny smiled toothsomely, and Horatia raised her slanted nose: Louisa took all of this pantomime to indicate their confirmation of the truth of what their mother said.

"I intend to make my peace with Lady Landor tomorrow," Lady Ellis continued enthusiastically, nodding her turbaned head and looking more than ever like a quill pen heavily overtopped with feathers. "After all, she *is* my relative by marriage, and although I did resent the fact that Alfred chose so young a wife, it is high time that bygones became bygones. Perhaps you will be good enough to tell her that, although I do not care to interrupt her tonight, she shall have a note from me tomorrow."

"And from me, as well," Mrs. Thrasher announced, shoving her way forward at the expense of the positions the three Miss Ellises had established. A rocket's glare cast a strange green pallor over the stout personage's face, making her look bilious. "I confess, my dear, to having been quite taken in. Sir Thomas spoke so easily on the matter of Lady Landor. . . . And then, of course, there was her appearance, which seemed to substantiate everything he said."

"And, of course, it suited you to believe it," Louisa retorted. "Mrs. Thrasher. Lady Ellis. I do not know whether or not Lady Landor will find it in her heart to forgive you. It is not my affair."

She spoke stiffly, hoping to warn them not to press her, for with her temper as uneven as it clearly was, Louisa did not know what she might or might not say given the opportunity.

"You must be proud that she is such a heroine," Lady Ellis said in her oily voice. "Why, I predict that Lady Landor will be so much in demand that she will never have a free afternoon or evening. I know that I intend . . ."

"Oh, but she must come to me first," Mrs. Thrasher exclaimed. "And, of course, the invitation will include you, Miss Rogers. How fortunate you are to have been connected with Lady Landor, after all."

"Your duplicity amazes me," Louisa exclaimed, no longer able to keep her temper under control. "Send me no invitations, ladies. You were so eager to hear the worst of her until the events of this evening showed you what side it would be sensible to be on. This—this hypocracy you practice may be the style. I am certain plain speaking is not—but I want no part of it. Do you hear?"

And with that she hurried along the path which ran beside the river, not able to go as fast as she wanted to because of the crowd. She cried out when she felt a hand on her arm.

"That was plainly spoken," Lord Cardross told her. There were no rockets at the moment, and he was in a shadow. She could not determine whether or not he mocked her. "They were shocked, but no doubt they will forgive you because of your relationship with Lady Landor."

"I do not want their forgiveness," Louisa told him, her eyes blazing. "And I do not want your kind concern. Clearly you do not understand what troubles me. Besides, it is my guess that now the matter of Sir Thomas has been taken care of, you will find other matters to occupy you. Now, sir, if you will let me go, I will join Miss Patterson. She, at least, understands."

Chapter Twenty

IT was Claire's idea that they go riding the next morning, and Louisa readily agreed.

"It will give you chance to be alone with your thoughts, if that is what you want," her friend had told her the night before as she had pressed Louisa's hands in parting. "So much has happened. And you seem disturbed. I will be with you for company, but if you want to be alone, I will understand."

It had been with some difficulty that Louisa had managed to persuade the groom Claire had brought with her that she and her friend could ride alone without the slightest difficulty. While she had been at the academy she had ridden daily, and Claire, when she was at her family estate in the country, often rode to the hounds.

Once they were inside the park the trees hid all the buildings, and Louisa, having ridden on ahead of Claire, was able to pretend that she was in the country again, that Lady Landor's problem never had concerned her, that she had never set eyes on Michelle Rioux and her brother, and had never met Lord Cardross. . . .

But no! She would not go too far. Cantering along the bridal path sidesaddle, with her gray skirts billowing in the wind and her black curls, left partly uncontrolled by the top hat she was wearing, blowing softly against her cheek, Louisa told herself that her stay in London had taught her something of value. And that, ironically enough, was that she could not endure to be chained to the demands of a small, elite society such as she had found here. Furthermore, she did not desire to be encircled by secrets, manipulated by people who had their private lives which she could not share.

She would not think of Claire's brother. She *would* not. And Claire must know it, for this morning she had not mentioned his name. What had she done? Louisa asked herself. Let him see her behaving as an unmanagable child for still another time, following impulse wildly and never once listening to her head? Besides, it was not that humiliation which made her bitter. She and Miss Patterson and all the others, including Claire and Lady Cardross, had been treated like children. Lady Landor would be given a bit more serious consideration, of course. After all, she was to give evidence against Sir Thomas. Then, of course, she would have served her purpose and could go back to being a giddy-headed doll again.

Even her father was guilty, Louisa told herself with a downcast heart. Flicking her riding crop lightly, she spurred the bay into a gallop, at the same time glancing behind her to see that Claire followed apace. How good it was of her to be content to keep her silent company, to wait until Louisa would want to talk.

Now, however, was a time to think. The night before, she had waited for her father to make her privy to what had been going on. But the captain's congratulations of Lady Landor had continued so unabated that Louisa had given up the attempt. She was, it seemed, to accept the situation as being de facto, ask no questions about anyone including her French acquaintances and the part they had played in all this. Well, let him keep his secrets, military or otherwise! As for Hugh and the duke, even though they knew no more about it than the ladies, they had adopted a knowledgeable manner, as gentlemen will in such affairs, and pretended to know all about it.

And what was she to do, Louisa considered? Riding rough in the park in the early morning might be one way of relieving her sense of oppression, but the relief would not last. What good would it do to confide in Claire, good friend though she was? It helped a little to remind herself that a least her father had not been forced to face Sir Thomas with pistols somewhere nearby in the early blush of morning. But nothing had been solved. Not really. It had been an odd coincidence that the very man her father had called out had been the one to be charged with spying on the enemy. Louisa reminded herself that she could take some thanks for that, since somehow the invitation to the duchess's party must have led Michelle Rioux and her brother to a trail leading to Sir Thomas. But in counting up the credits, it was well to remember that even though Lady Landor was now, apparently, to be a heroine with no more scandal spread about her, she would be apt to lead Louisa's father a merry chase.

Very well, Louisa told herself, bending her head into the wind and driving the horse until she felt that she were flying. Very well! She would begin to make her own choices. Her father might like to think that she would simply come to London and behave like everybody else. Think herself lucky to find someone with money and a title to marry her. Spend her life planning entertainments and exchanging on-dits with her friends. But she had other plans. She would ask Miss Patterson to give her a position as one of her teachers at the academy. There was no reason at all why she should not be a bluestocking if she wanted.

The idea gave her fresh courage, and she was just slowing the bay to a different pace when she heard the sound of hooves close behind her; turning, expecting to see Claire, she found that she was being closely followed by Claire's brother instead.

For a single moment it came into her mind to lead him a race. But that would be childish, indeed, she told herself, still tempted by the notion that perhaps she might win. But then she tried to make herself believe that it was only accident that he should meet her here. Perhaps he rode in the park every morning. But if that were the case, Claire would know it. She must have deliberately led Louisa into this trap. At his suggestion? Louisa turned to stare at Lord Cardross angrily as he came riding up beside her.

"Did you arrange this, sir?" she demanded. "Did you use your sister to get me here?"

Looking back, Louisa saw that Claire had fallen very far behind. Indeed, she was dismounting and seemed about to walk her horse instead of ride him, no doubt to avoid coming too close. How could she have done this? How could she have acted as his agent?

"I confess that Claire did agree to help me," Lord Cardross told her. "You parted from me angrily the night before, and as a close friend of your father . . ."

That was it then! Louisa did not bother to listen to anything else he said. At least that is what she told herself. What did it matter what he said when he only thought of her as her father's daughter? What did it matter that he mounted his horse so well or that he looked unduly handsome in his blue coat and his shining Hessian boots? And then her ear was caught by the sound of Lady Landor's name.

"She has agreed to my plan," the young viscount told the dark-haired girl as they cantered on together. "I saw her this morning and she agreed."

"Nonsense," Louisa replied quickly. "I mean to say, you could not have seen Lady Landor. She never shows herself, if possible, before noon and certainly not at this hour. Why, it is not even nine."

"All the same, I saw her," he replied with a hint of laughter in his voice. "Granted that she was in dishabille."

"And just what plan was it she agreed to?" Louisa demanded. "I do not think it likely that you would pay attention to whether she agreed or not. Either you or my father for that matter."

"You make more sense than you imagine, Miss Rogers," Lord Cardross said with a smile. "Thanks again to Miss Patterson. We had a talk about you, and I hope you do not mind."

"Mind!" Louisa exploded. "Of course I mind considerably. What right had she—had you . . . Why, I do not know what to make of any of this. You will oblige me, sir, by making sense of what is going on."

"I only mentioned Miss Patterson because she explained to me why you were so angry last night at Vauxhall Garden," he said quickly. "And, although you may not believe me, that was precisely what I had guessed was going on inside your head."

"My pretty head," Louisa corrected him dryly. "Surely that is what you meant to say, sir. That is one of the many ways you gentlemen like to condescend."

For a moment Lord Cardross looked very grim. "I intend to prove to you, Miss Rogers, that I do not make a practice of condescending, whatever you may care to think. And I realize now that it may take some doing to overcome your resistance. Your headmistress said that you were stubborn and hard-headed, on occasion."

"I cannot think what possessed her to talk about me like that," Louisa fretted under her breath. "Well, sir, when you are done complimenting me, perhaps we can go on to discuss your plan, the one Lady Landor approved of. You will forgive me if I laugh."

"Laugh all you want to," Lord Cardross told her. "I think I shall have the last one, all the same. If you will accompany me back to Grosvenor Square, we should find that your father has arrived there. I sent a message to him before I came out riding after you. Miss Patterson is to be included because she can be trusted."

Louisa turned her blue eyes on him. "Oh, we are to hear secrets, are we? As a special favor."

She would have gone on had it not been that something in his eyes told her she had said enough. And, of course, she could not expect him to put up with her taunting. Particularly when he clearly thought he was doing her a favor. What was there about the gentleman, Louisa wondered, which made her behave so badly?

"I will be interested to hear anything you can tell us about Sir Thomas Tigger, sir," she said, turning her horse's head. "That is what we will be discussing, I presume."

"Your presumption is well taken," he told her, and she noticed that his face was drawn in set lines.

When they reached the spot where Claire was standing by her horse, Louisa slipped down from the saddle and embraced her friend. "My first thought was to be angry," she told her. "And I cannot promise that I will not be in the end. But not with you, I think."

It was little enough to say, but it was sufficient. Claire's relieved expression told Louisa that she had been afraid that when it was discovered she had arranged this meeting there would be a line drawn between them. Now she must know that whatever conflict Louisa had with her brother, that could never happen.

Lord Cardross had made his plans well. The groom he had brought with him was waiting at the edge of the park by Park Lane to escort Claire back home. As for Louisa, she rode beside him back to Grosvenor Square, neither of them volunteering another word.

They were being awaited by the little group gathered in the Oriental drawing room, with its cabinets of black and gold, the vases with the dragons, and the brilliant carpet. Lady Landor, to Louisa's surprise, was no longer in dishabille. Wearing a red and white striped morning dress and with her hair dressed high, she managed to look very distinguished and not a little pleased with herself. As for the captain, he was wearing his uniform as he had the night before and looked very dashing in his black boots, white breeches, double-breasted red jacket with white-fringed epaulets on the shoulders, and high collar over his cravat. His black, tricornered hat with its red and white feather was lying on one of the gilted tables which dotted the room. He stood near the mantel beside the chair where Miss Patterson, neat in grey and white, sat with her hands folded in her lap.

"So, you have found her, have you?" the captain said to the young viscount. "It is not wise for a young girl to go out alone for a ride in London, my dear Louisa. But I expect that you knew that and did it all the same."

"I am sorry if I worried you, Papa," Louisa said dutifully, wondering if that was what made him look so very serious.

"Come and sit down, my dear," her father went on. "Miles. There is claret there if you wish to take a glass. Now, my dear Louisa, I want you to know, straight off, that I am doing this at this gentleman's request. Last night, after we left you ladies, he convinced me that it would be best. And, I must agree, that after having Miss Patterson express your viewpoint to me this morning . . ."

"You must forgive me, Louisa," the headmistress said calmly, "but I thought it best your father know. It would not have suited you to become a cynic. Not at such a tender age."

Captain Rogers looked at Miss Patterson with clear affection. "You are a wise woman," he said gently, "and you know how much I have always trusted you. With that in mind, I will not swear you to secrecy. It will not be necessary, in your case either, Louisa. You may be impulsive in some things, but where military affairs which are my responsibility are concerned, I know you will be silent."

Louisa stared at him, bewildered. Something had changed. Something was very different. She sensed it, and she knew it was important. But she did not know how to put her finger on it.

"I understand," her father went on, "that you were angry because Sir Thomas's arrest was carried off with no real explanation of the part we played, Miles and I; that you felt, in general, that too much had been going on about which you had not been kept informed. Further, that you attributed this failure of communication to the fact that you are female and therefore due to be the subject of every sort of discrimination."

That was, Louisa thought, more clearly put than she had been able to state it herself. "Yes, Papa," she said in a way which did not commit her far. "But, of course, if military secrets are involved . . ."

Lord Cardross laughed, and Louisa was not certain that it was a happy sound. "You have been responsible for this meeting, Miss Rogers," he told her. "You would be doing us all a favor if you did not turn around and say you do not want to hear what your father has to tell you. I arranged this because I thought it only fair. I have not changed my mind. Besides, when you know the truth, you may look at things quite differently.''

She would still return to the country with Miss Patterson, Louisa promised herself. Nothing that could be said here today would change that. After this was over, she would talk to the head-mistress seriously about providing her with a teaching post.

"The fact is," Lady Landor said quite suddenly, as though she could not wait any longer, "that I have been spying for the English government for well over a year. Me, a spy! Imagine! Even now, sometimes, I have to pinch myself to believe it."

A Japanese tapestry hung on the wall behind the chair in which Lady Landor was sitting. Louisa found herself staring at it with grim determination. The tapestry showed a garden party. Four la-dies wearing brightly patterned robes were talking together while a single man sat on the floor of what appeared to be an outdoor room and stared at a row of giant flowers which were quite unlike any Louisa had ever seen.

"La," she heard Lady Landor say. "Can you say nothing, Miss Patterson? Louisa, why do you look so strange? I thought you would be proud of me."

It all came out then. It seemed that Captain Rogers and Lord Cardross had become friends when they had shared a mission to the Turkish empire three years ago.

"Miles makes delicate inquries about certain political matters," the captain explained, "and reports to a committee working with the House of Lords where, of course, he has a seat. At one point, our commissions overlapped, and we became acquainted."

"We were both interested in the activities of a certain Sir Thomas Tigger," Lord Cardross went on. "He made a point of leaving England regularly and visiting certain cities. We were told that he fancied himself a world traveler, but we were certain that there was more to it than that. There were reasons . . ."

"Which there will be no need for us to go into," Captain Rogers said briskly. "However, in the various cities that Sir Thomas always visited, we contacted people who could keep an eye on his activities."

"People who could be trusted," Lady Landor said proudly. "Lord Cardross came to Florence. He saw at once that Sir Thomas would never suspect someone like me. And he saw at once that I was only giddy when I wanted to be, did you not, sir? It was dur-

ing my poor husband's last illness. I knew that I should want to return to London later. And, I also knew that Lady Ellis had a spiteful tongue. Lord Cardross and I made a bargain. I was to return to
London when the time came, under the best of all possible conditions to promote me socially.''

Louisa stared at her father incredulously. ''Am I to believe from
that,'' she demanded, ''that your so-called engagement to Lady
Landor was all part of a plot?''

She saw Miss Patterson stiffen when she said that, as though the
headmistress had had a shock and, knowing only too well what she
must be feeling, Louisa went and took her hand.

''We were to meet on a boat in the Bay of Biscay,'' Lady
Landor said happily. ''I was to know Captain Rogers's identity for
certain when he presented me with an ivory fan.''

''How could you do it, father?'' Louisa demanded. ''To have
put a false face to the world is bad enough, but to have deceived
me, as well!''

''I made that one of my conditions,'' Lady Landor said. ''No
one except Lord Cardross was to know. Oh, we had our stipula-
tions on both sides. I was to pretend a slight malady after Alfred
died to keep me in the city until Sir Thomas had come and gone. I
noted whom he talked to, as usual, and then, I expect, I became
too bold and put him off so absolutely that he turned against me.''

''This is a strange tale,'' Louisa heard Miss Patterson murmur.
''And how are Mademoiselle Rioux and her brother involved?
Does this all come together, after all?''

It was the same question Louisa wanted to ask, but first she
knew it was time to add an explanation. ''They came to me and
asked me to introduce them,'' she told her father. ''When Mademoiselle Rioux explained how some people in society give information for the support of Napoleon, I thought you would want me
to help them.''

''I have never met Mademoiselle Rioux and her brother,'' Captain Rogers told her. ''It was Lord Cardross who discovered that
they were making Sir Thomas the subject of their investigation,
too. It took a few days to sort the matter out. The French community in this country has its own ways. But Cardross was able to
convince them we should work together and share the prize.''

''That was when you went away so mysteriously,'' Louisa murmured. ''That was why Michelle and her brother disappeared at
the same time.''

Lord Cardross nodded, his dark eyes intent on hers. "As your father says, it was necessary to persuade them that if we were to share our information, we might remove Sir Thomas from his unfortunate occupation earlier than either of us could do alone. You have seen with your own eyes at Vauxhall just how well they cooperated in the end."

"It has been an extraordinary case in many ways," Captain Rogers added. "In the ordinary way, people who give us information either do it for patriotic reasons, with no expectation of reward, or they accept a small fee for their toubles. Lady Landor, however, wanted something quite different. We were to provide her with respectability, Lord Cardross through the patronage of his mother and sister and I—well—as her fiancé. As soon as she heard I had a daughter, she wanted you with her."

"To lend more respectability?" Louisa murmured.

"I wanted the companionship," Lady Landor told her. "And I wanted to help you with your coming out, just as I told you. Of course, when I began to realize that serious charges must have been made against me . . ."

"I tried to keep them from you," Louisa said.

Lady Landor rose and came toward the girl, pausing by one of the green lacquer cabinets which stood on either side of a long window. "I know you did now, and I am grateful," she said quite simply. "And I do not want you to think badly of your father for deceiving you. It happened that the people Sir Thomas saw in Florence were important. And, as a consequence, what I had to tell was important, too. It must have been worth the trouble it caused him, or your father never would have agreed to the pretense. And he has been a perfect gentleman, although we would never suit one another in reality."

"And Sir Thomas's stories?" Louisa demanded. "Tell me, were they true?"

"La, how they took me by surprise!" Lady Landor exclaimed. "I expected to have to overcome my sister-in-law's malice, but nothing more. And then, when I turned him against me . . . Ah, well. They were an exaggeration, my dear Louisa. I may have flirted high and low, but I was never unfaithful to my husband. And Alfred never minded, particularly as I never flirted in his company. It is very difficult, I found, to flirt . . ."

"When you do not know the language," Miss Patterson said dryly.

"Precisely so," Lady Landor said, laughing. "How well you understand me."

"One final question," Louisa said quickly. "Why did you swoon when you saw Sir Thomas here with me? For that matter, Lord Cardross, why did you allow me to go through that interview with the gentleman when you knew . . ."

"I knew nothing, Miss Rogers," he said gently, "except that, in time, Sir Thomas would be arrested. But I did not know how, in the meantime, we were to overcome the impression that his wild stories were making on society. There was a chance that you could convince him to be silent, and I thought that you should take it."

"As for my swoon," Lady Landor declared, "I declare, child, I fancied he had found me out and had come here to make trouble for me. Had you been in my place, you would have felt the same."

"Have we made a clear case, Miss Rogers?" Lord Cardross asked Louisa, his dark eyes intent on her face. "Your father and I are both in secret service for this country, although not quite in the same way. Lady Landor was enlisted to help us, which she did in exchange for the promise that both your father and I would lend our assistance to establishing her in the *haut ton*. The information she was able to give us about Sir Thomas Tigger needed substantiation. And that took time."

"It explains your sudden absence?"

"Precisely, Miss Rogers. After my return we simply needed to choose time and place. I must confess, however, that it might not have happened as soon as it did had it not been for two circumstances."

"The duel was one, I think," Miss Patterson suggested. "Was that part of your secret schemes?"

The captain shook his grizzled head. Looking at him, Louisa realized how relieved she was that he was not to marry Lady Landor after all. She had tried her best to accept his decision, but there had always been a reservation.

"The duel was forced on me," he said. "I would not have allowed the gentleman to approach me if I had realized how vicious his stories would be. Other gentlemen heard him tell them to me. I had no recourse but to call him out. It would have aroused suspicion otherwise. Besides, my part of the bargain was to protect your reputation, madam," he added, glancing in Lady Landor's direction.

"Clearly, however," Lord Cardross said, "the duel could not be allowed to happen, which meant the arrest had to take place at once."

"Miles was responsible for pulling strings at Whitehall to get me out of that awkward situation," the captain said. "But there was another reason for haste," he added, clearing his throat and glancing at Lady Landor. "The fact is, madam, that when, under the influence of laudanum, you made open accusations aimed at Sir Thomas, it was necessary for us to move at once before word got out, as it might have done, and he made his escape. It was fortunate that you happened to say what you did in the company of Lord Cardross."

"I confess to thinking that what she said was very strange," Miss Patterson told him. "But then I thought the drug had left her confused."

"Well, as for that," Lady Landor said complaisantly, "I believe I did very well, all the same. And now that it is known that I assisted the war effort, I am to be a heroine. That suits me very well, indeed. I shall be magnanimous to the extreme. When I give my first soiree, which will be very soon, I will make a point of inviting Lady Ellis and her poor daughters. I may even help them find husbands. After all, we are related. And Mrs. Thrasher. I will invite her, as well. Everyone will see that, in victory, I can be gracious."

Her liquid brown eyes looked past them into a bright future, and Lord Cardross drew Louisa to one side. "Now do you see why we could say nothing last night with all the others about?" he asked her. "The role your father and I play in serving the country must never be that clearly understood. It was no slur on you or on ladies in general which kept us silent. And Lady Landor is right. She *is* a heroine of sorts. There is room in this society for ladies to be something more than you sketched them as being last night at Vauxhall Gardens."

It mattered to him what she thought, Louisa realized with delight. Why, she had been wrong about the way he thought of her all along. The books she and Miss Patterson had poured over had not been enough to teach her what she needed to know about people. Certainly they had not really told her about love.

"Have no fear, sir," Louisa said, indulging herself in a smile characterized by a certain archness, "I am no longer angry. It was a tempest in a teapot. Nothing more."

"Ah, but it was a charming tempest," he told her with a slow smile. "Shall we talk about it? May I dare to hope that we have a good deal to say to one another."

"I do not think there will ever be an end to our conversation, sir," Louisa told him. "And so we must hurry and make a start."

Chapter Twenty-One

ALL of London's *haut ton* seemed to be at Lady Landor's party, which she was holding in the ballroom on the third floor of the house on Grosvenor Square. Glittering chandeliers showered crystal-reflected brightness onto the milling crowd, and the air was thick with the scent of flowers and perfume. Ladies with their hair dressed in extravagant fashions wore their stylish gowns with a flare, lending every color of the rainbow to the scene. Gentlemen in evening dress rivaled one another with the elaborateness of their cravats. There was a rumor that Beau Brummell himself was in attendance, causing not a few necks to crane.

As for their hostess, she was graciousness itself as she stood at the head of the winding stairs and greeted the members of society who had flocked to her soiree. Everyone knew the way she had served her country, and there was no end to the congratulations showered on her, all of which she received as being her due. As for the breaking of her engagement with Captain Rogers, she dealt with it in an expedient way.

"Tell everyone that I am fancy-free again," she would say at intervals as her guests passed by her. "The dear captain and I have come to an agreement not to wed. I am too busy to make another marriage just at present, you understand."

And then she would murmur something about international intrigue, quite as though that was her forte. Indeed, Louisa thought, it might be that she believed it was. Certainly, earlier, when Maria had helped her make her elaborate toilette, she had had the Italian abigail call Louisa three times and Miss Patterson twice to ask them if she looked sufficiently mysterious and spylike in her gown of midnight-blue velvet with diamonds sparkling in her chestnut hair. Even Maria seemed to have caught some of her mistress's enthusiasm. At least she was not as dour as usual and actually nodded her head once in response to some comment of Louisa's,

157

something she would not ordinarily do, indicating as it did that she understood what the girl was saying.

Now, looking more flamboyantly beautiful than usual, Lady Landor sent an order that the musicians should start the music and indicated that, rather than lead the dancing, she intended to circulate about the room.

"She cannot get enough of the adulation," Lord Cardross observed to Louisa as they stood together in an alcove, she decked in primrose muslin cut low at the bodice and high at the sleeve, with primrose ribbons in her dark curls, and the young viscount elegant in black. "Ah, well, there is no harm that she should have it. If it suits her, all the better."

"I think it suits my father well enough," Louisa told him, nodding in the direction of the dance floor where Captain Rogers was preparing to lead Miss Patterson in a waltz. At Louisa's command, the headmistress had not only left her gold-rimmed spectacles off this evening, but she had loosened her hair until it hung in tendrils about her neck and forehead. Indeed, she had agreed to borrowing one of Louisa's dresses, a fetching affair of pale blue silk which suited her very well indeed. Louisa could tell by the way the captain was looking at her that he had discovered a loveliness about her which he had never seen before.

"I think he has always been fonder of her than he knew," Lord Cardross replied. "For the last two years, at least, he has come back from visiting you at the academy with one commendation after another about her. Had they not all been of an academic nature, I would have thought long ago that they might make a match of it."

"It will be quite perfect for them," Louisa told him. "She can keep her school, and he will be off and away on his travels, and when he is at home . . ."

"Life is one long, delightful story for you," Lord Cardross teased her. "With happy endings around every corner, I hope."

"I would not have thought so a week ago," Louisa murmured. "Indeed, I was quite certain then that the reverse would be so. For example, I was afraid that Lady Landor might make your sister and Mr. Trever quarrel."

He smiled at that. "Claire realized, at last, that Lady Landor means nothing by her flirtations."

"She can no more help herself from doing that than she can keep herself from breathing," Louisa declared with conviction.

"That is what I told the Duchess. And the Duke sees it, as well, now. He will not let himself be carried away in future."

And, indeed, just as she spoke, the Duchess and the Duke of Taxton took the floor. The lady wore an expression which had something of triumph in it as her rotund husband whirled her about. Once having danced with Lady Landor, he could not claim any disability to do so, leaving the duchess with an ace in hand. Claire, radiant in primrose yellow silk, came dancing by in Hugh Trever's arms and blew her brother and Louisa a kiss. And who should follow that couple but Mademoiselle Rioux and Claude, the latter much less dour than usually seemed to be the case and his sister elegantly gay.

Meanwhile, Lady Landor was making her way about the room, clearly rejoicing at having so many friends about her. Louisa saw her gather up Lady Ellis and her daughters and herd them about until, somehow or other, Patience, Fanny, and Horatia, eyes, teeth, slanted nose and all, had acquired partners, three astounded-looking young gentlemen who soon found themselves being whirled about the floor with enthusiasm which, no doubt, made up for lack of art. Whereupon Lady Ellis looked even more like a quill pen than usual in her pride, and Lady Landor left her to exchange a word with Mrs. Thrasher who appeared to be puffing and panting out compliments at a very great rate indeed.

"Hypocrisy does not trouble her, I see," Lord Cardross observed and smiled to hear Louisa laughing. Then they were joined by his mother, who called Louisa "my dear" in a very confidential sort of way and told her that she and Miles should be dancing like the others.

"People should see the two of you together," she told them. "Then, you see, they will not be at all surprised when they see the announcement of your engagement tomorrow in *The Gazette*."

"As long as I am with you, I do not care whether we dance or not," Lord Cardross told Louisa as they approached the dance floor. "Particularly since there is such a crush."

"If we could slip away downstairs," Louisa told him, "we could take a stroll about the garden. I think the moon is full tonight. But do you think we should? You know how little it takes to make people talk."

"I know," he told her in a murmur, "but do we really care?"

And so they slipped away, down the curved staircase. Only Lady Landor saw them go. She smiled and took the credit for it.

Later, happening to glance down from an open window at the back, she saw them dancing in the moonlight and determined not to say a word about it.

"My lips are sealed," she said to no one in particular and, waving her ivory fan, went on her merry way. And, in the garden far below, the two figures waltzing along the rose-rimmed path to the distant strains of music, disappeared into the shadow and were lost.